WHAT COMES AROUND

Also by Ted Bell

FICTION

Phantom
Warlord
Tsar
Spy
Pirate
Assassin
Hawke

STORIES

Crash Dive

CHILDREN'S BOOKS

The Time Pirate
Nick of Time

WHAT COMES AROUND

An Alex Hawke Novella

TED BELL

WILLIAM MORROW IMPULSE
An Imprint of HarperCollins Publishers

Excerpt from *Warriors* copyright © 2014 by Theodore A. Bell.

EPub Edition FEBRUARY 2014 ISBN: 9780062283214
Print Edition ISBN: 9780062322036

10 9 8 7 6 5 4

WHAT COMES AROUND

Back in Hook's day, portraits of the great man beamed benevolence down at you from every wall of every classroom. He was our Father, the Father of our country. Your country! Why, if you had told young Cam back then that in just one or two generations, the General himself would have been scrubbed clean from the history—why, he would have—

"What are you thinking about, dear?" his wife said, interrupting his dark reverie at the breakfast table later that morning. Gillian was perusing what he'd always referred to as the "Women's Sports Section." Sometimes known as the bridal pages in the Sunday edition of the *New York Times*. Apparently, it was the definitive weekly "Who's Who" of who'd married whom last week. For all those out there who, like his wife of sixty years, were still keeping score, he supposed.

"You're frowning, dear," she said.

"Hmm."

He scratched his grizzled chin and sighed, gazing out at the forests of green trees reaching down to the busy harbor. On the surface, all was serene. But even now a mud-caked munchkin wielding a blue Frisbee bat advanced stealthily up the hill, stalking one of his old chocolate Labs sleeping in the foreground.

"Will you look at that?" he mused.

Gillian put the paper down and peered at him over the toaster.

"What is it, dear?"

"Oh, nothing. It's July, you know," he said, rapping sharply on the window to alert his dog of the impending munchkin attack.

"July? What about it?"

"July is the cruelest month," he said, not looking up from the Book Review, "Not April. July. That's all."

"Oh, good heavens," she said, and snatched away her paper.

"Precisely," he said but got no reply.

Dismissed, he stood and leaned across the table to kiss his wife's proffered cheek.

"It's your own damn fault, Cam Hooker," she said, stroking his own freshly shaved cheek. "If you'd relent for once in your life, if you'd only let them have a television, just one! That old RCA black and white portable up in the attic would do nicely. Or even one of those handheld computer thingies, whatever they're called. Silence would reign supreme in this house once more. But no. Not you."

"A television? In *this* house?" he said. "Oh, no. Not in this house. Never!"

Grabbing his smokes, his newspapers and his canvas sail bag and swinging out into the backyard, slamming the screen door behind him, he headed down the sloping green lawn to his dock. The old Hooker property, some fifteen acres of it, was right at the tip of Crabtree Point, with magnificent views of the Fox Islands Thorofare inlet and the Camden Hills to the west. He was the fifth generation of Hookers to summer on this island, not that anyone cared a whit

CHAPTER 1

THE BRIGHT BLUE waters of Penobscot Bay beckoned, and Cam Hooker paused to throw open his dressing room window. Glorious morning, all right. Sunlight sparkled out on the bay, flashing white sea-birds wheeled and dove above. He took a deep breath of pine-scented Maine air and assessed the morning's weather. Sunny now, but threatening skies. Fresh breeze out of the east, and a moderate chop, fifteen knots sustained, maybe gusting to thirty. Barometer falling, increased cloudiness, possible thunderheads moving in from the west by mid-morning. Chance of rain showers later on, oh, sixty to seventy per cent, give or take.

Perfect.

Certainly nothing an old salt like Cameron Hooker couldn't handle.

It was Sunday, praise the Lord, his favorite day of

the week. The day he got to take himself, his *New York Times,* his Marlboros, and whatever tattered paperback spy novel he was currently headlong into reading for the third time (an old Alistair MacLean) out on his boat for a few tranquil hours of peace and quiet and bliss.

Hooker had sailed her, his black ketch *Maracaya,* every single Sunday morning of his life, for nigh on forty years now, rain or shine, sleet, hail, or snow.

Man Alone. A singleton. Solitary.

It was high summer again, and summer meant grandchildren by the dozen. Toddlers, rugrats, and various ragamuffins running roughshod throughout his rambling old seaside cottage on North Haven Island. Haven? Hah! Up and down the back stairs they rumbled, storming through his cherished rose gardens, dashing inside and out, marching through his vegetable patches like jackbooted thugs and even invading the sanctuary of his library, all the while shouting at peak decibels some mysterious new battle cry, "Huzzah! Huzzah!" picked up God knew where.

It was the Revolutionary War victory cheer accorded to General George Washington, he knew that, but this intellectually impoverished gizmo generation had not a clue who George Washington was! Of that much, at least, he was certain.

You knew you were down in the deep severe when not a single young soul in your entire clan had the remotest clue who the hell the Father of Our Country was!

about such things anymore. His ancestor, Captain Osgood Hooker, had first come here from Boston to "recuperate from the deleterious effects of the confinements of city life," as he'd put it in a letter Cam had found in a highboy in the dining room. Traditions, history, common sense and common courtesy, things like that, all gone to hell or by the wayside. Hell, they were trying to get rid of Christmas! Some goddamn school district in Ohio had banned the singing of "Silent Night." "Silent Night"!

He could see her out there at the far end of the dock when he crested the hill. Just the sight of her never failed to move him. His heart skipped a beat, literally, every time she hove into view.

Maracaya was her name.

She was an old Alden-design ketch and he'd owned her for longer than time. Forty feet on the waterline, wooden hull, gleaming black Awlgrip, with a gold cove stripe running along her flank beneath the gunwales. Her decks were teak, her spars were Sitka-spruce, and she was about as yar as any damn boat currently plying the waters of coastal Maine, in his humble opinion.

Making his way down the hill to the sun-dappled water, he couldn't take his eyes off her.

She'd never looked better.

He had a young kid this summer, sophomore at Yale, living down here in the boathouse. The boy helped him keep *Maracaya* in proper Bristol fashion. She was a looker, all right, but she was a goer, too.

He'd won the Block Island Race on her back in '87, and then the Nantucket Opera Cup the year after that. Now, barely memories, just dusty trophies on the mantel in some people's goddamn not-so-humble opinion.

"'Morning, Skipper," the crew-cut blond kid said, popping his head up from the companionway. "Coffee's on below, sir. You're good to go."

"Thanks, Ben, good on ya, mate."

"Good day for it, sir," the young fellow said, looking up at the big blue sky with his big white smile. He was a good kid, this Ben Sparhawk. Sixth-generation North Haven, dad and granddad were both hard-working lobstermen. Came from solid Maine stock, too. Men from another time, men who could toil at being a fisherman, a farmer, sailor, lumberman, a shipwright, and a quarryman, all rolled into one. And master of all.

Salt of the earth, formerly salt of the sea, Thoreau had called such men.

Ben was a history major at New Haven, on a full scholarship. He had a head on his shoulders, he did, and he used it. He came up from the galley below and quickly moved to the portside bow, freeing the forward, spring, and aft mooring lines before leaping easily from the deck down onto the dock.

"Prettiest boat in the harbor she is, sir," Ben said, looking at her gleaming mahogany topsides with some pride.

"Absofuckinlutely, son," Cam said, laughing out

loud at his good fortune, another glorious day await-
ing him out there on the water. He was one of the
lucky ones and he knew it. A man in good health,
of sound mind, and looking forward to the precious
balance of his time here on earth, specifically in the
great state of Maine.

Cam Hooker was semiretired from the Agency
now. He'd been Director under George H.W. Bush
and had had a good run. Under his watch, the CIA
was a tightly run ship. No scandals, no snafus, no
bullshit, just a solid record of intelligence successes
around the world. He was proud of his service to his
country and it pained him to see the condition it was
in now. Diminished, that was the word, goddamnit.
How could the bastards, all of them, let this happen
to his magnificent country?

He shook off such thoughts, leaving them well
ashore as he stepped aboard his boat. He went aft
and climbed down into the cockpit. First thing he
did, he kicked his topsiders off so he could feel the
warm teak decks on the soles of his feet. He felt
better already. Smell that air!

Ben Sparhawk had thoughtfully removed and
stowed the sail cover from the mainsail. Cam grabbed
the main halyard, took a couple of turns around the
starboard winch and started grinding, the big mainsail blooming with fresh Maine air as it rose majesti-
cally up the stick.

Some days, when there was no wind to speak of,
he'd crank up the old Universal diesel, a forty-two-

horsepower lump of steel that had served him well over the decades. Now, with a freshening breeze, he winched the main up, loosing the sheets and letting her sails flop in the wind. The jib was roller-furling, one of his few concessions to modernity, and at his advancing age, a godsend for its ease of use. He also had a storm trysail rigged that he'd deploy when he got out beyond the harbor proper.

"Shove that bow off for me, Ben, willya?" he said, putting the helm over and sheeting in the main.

"Aye, Skipper," the kid said, and moments later he was pointed in the right direction and moving away from the dock toward the Thorofare running between North Haven and Vinalhaven islands.

He turned to wave good-bye to the youngster, saw him smiling and waving back with both hands. He was surprised to find his old blue eyes suddenly gone all blurry with tears.

By God, he wished he'd had a son like that.

CHAPTER 2

HE THREADED HIS way, tacking smartly through the teeming Thorofare. It was crowded as hell, always was this time of year, especially this Fourth of July weekend. Boats and yachts of every description hove into view: the Vinalhaven ferry steaming stolidly across, knockabouts and dinghies, a lovely old Nat Herreshoff gaff-headed Bar Harbor 30; and here came one of the original Internationals built in Norway, sparring with a Luders; and even a big Palmer Johnson stink-pot anchored just off Foy Brown's Yard, over a hundred feet long he'd guess, with New York Yacht Club burgees emblazoned on her smokestack. Pretty damn fancy for these parts, if you asked him.

As was his custom, once he was in open water he had put her hard over, one mile from shore, and headed for the pretty little harbor over on the mainland at Rockport. Blowing like stink out here now.

Clouding up. Front moving in for damn sure. He stood to windward at the helm, both hands on the big wheel, his feet planted wide, and sang a few bars of his favorite sailor's ditty, sung to the tune of an old English ballad "Robin on the Moor":

> "It was a young captain on Cranberry
>   Isles did dwell;
> He took the schooner Arnold, one you
>   all know well.
> She was a tops'l schooner and hailed
>   from Calais, Maine;
> They took a load from Boston to cross
>   the raging main—"

The words caught in his throat.

He'd seen movement down in the galley below. Not believing his eyes, he looked again. Nothing. Perhaps just a light shadow from a porthole sliding across the cabin floor as he fell off the wind a bit? Nothing at all; and yet it had spooked him there for a second, but he—

"Hello, Cam," a strange-looking man said, suddenly making himself visible at the foot of the steps down in the galley. And then he was climbing up into the cockpit.

"What the hell?" Cam said, startled.

"Relax. I don't bite."

"Who the hell are you? And what the hell are you doing aboard my boat?"

Cam eased the main a bit to reduce the amount of heel and moved higher to the windward side of the helm station. He planted himself and bent his knees, ready for any false move from years of habit in the military and later as a Special Agent out in the field. The stranger made no move other than to plop himself down on a faded red cushion on the leeward side of the cockpit and cross his long legs.

"You don't recognize me? I'm hurt. Maybe it's the long hair and the beard. Here, I know. Look at the eyes, Cam, you can always remember the eyes."

Cam looked.

Was that Spider, for God's sake?

It couldn't be. But it was. Spider Payne, for crissakes. A guy who'd worked for him at CIA briefly the year before he retired. Good agent, a guy on the way up. He'd lost track of him long ago . . . and now? There'd been some kind of trouble but he couldn't recall exactly what.

"Spider, sure, sure, I recognize you," Cam said, keeping his voice as even as he could manage. "What in God's name is going on?"

"I knew this might freak you out. You know, if I just showed up on the boat like this. Sorry. I drove all night from Boston, then came over to the island on the ferry from Rockland last night. Parked my truck at Foy Brown's boatyard and went up to that little inn, the Nebo Lodge. Fully booked, not a bed to be had, wouldn't you know. Forgot it was the Fourth weekend. Stupid, I guess."

"Spider, you know this is highly goddamn unprofessional. Showing up unannounced like this. Uninvited. Are you all right? What's this all about?"

"How I found you, you mean?"

"*Why* you found me, Spider."

"Well, I remembered you always had a picture of a sailboat in your office at Langley. An oil painting. A black boat at a dock below your summer house in Maine. I even remembered the boat's name. *Maracaya*. So, when I couldn't get a room, I went downstairs to the bar there and had a few beers. Asked around about a boat called *Maracaya*. One old guy said, 'Ayuh. Alden ketch. She's moored out to the Hooker place, out to the end of Crabtree Point.' And here I am."

"No. Not here you fucking are, you idiot. How'd you get aboard? I've got a kid, looks after the boat. He'd never let you aboard."

"Cam, c'mon. It was four in the morning. Everyone was asleep. I climbed aboard and slept in the sail locker up forward. Say, it's blowing pretty good out here! Twenty knots? Think you should put in a reef?"

"Spider, you better tell me quick why you're here or you're swimming back. I am dead serious."

"I sent you a letter. A while back. You remember that? I asked for your help. I was in a little trouble with the French government. Arrested by the French for kidnapping and suspicion of murder. No body, no proof. But. Sentenced to thirty years for kidnapping a known Arab terrorist off the streets of Paris. Guy believed responsible for the Metro bombing that killed thirty Parisians in 2011. I was the number two guy in our Paris station, Cam! Operating within the law. Rendition was what we did then."

"Come to the point. I don't need all this history."

"I'd had a brilliant career. Not a blemish. And, when I got in trouble, the Agency threw me under the bus."

"The Agency, Spider, had nothing to do with it. That decision came down out of the White House. It may surprise you to learn that the President was more concerned about our relationship with one of our most powerful European allies than you. It was a delicate time. You're a victim of bad timing."

"My whole fucking life is destroyed because of bad timing?"

"I'm sorry about that. But it's got nothing to do with me. I retired prior to 9/11, remember? Frankly? I never approved of rendition in the first place. Enhanced interrogation. Abu Ghraib. All those 'black funds' you had at your disposal. Not the way we played the game, son. Not in my day."

"Look. I asked you to help me. I've yet to get a response, Cam. So now I'm here. In person. To ask you again. Right now. Will you help me? They ruined my life! I lost everything. My job, my shitty little farm in Aix-en-Provence. My wife took the children and disappeared. Now there's an international warrant for my arrest by the French government and my own country won't step in, Cam. All my savings gone to lawyers on appeal. I'm broke, Cam. I'm finished. Look at me. I'm falling out the window."

"Jesus Christ, Spider. What do you want? Money?"

"I want help."

"Fuck you."

"Really?"

"You screwed up, mister. Big-time. You jumped the shark, pal. You're not my problem."

"Really? You don't think I'm your problem, Cam? Are you sure about that?"

Spider stood up and took a step closer to the helm. Cam turned his cold blue eyes on him, eyes that had cowed far tougher men than this one by a factor of ten.

"Are you threatening me, son? I see it in your eyes. You think I may be getting a little long in the tooth, don't you, pal, but I'll rip your beating heart out, believe me."

"That's your response, then. You want me to beg? I come to you on bended knee, humbly, to beseech you for help. And you say you'll rip my heart out?"

The man was weeping.

"Listen, Spider. You're obviously upset. You need help, yes. But not from me. You need to see someone. A specialist. I can help you do that. I'll even pay for it. Look here. I'm going to flip her around now and head back to the dock. I'll see that you get proper care. Uncleat that mainsheet, will you, and prepare to come about. It's really blowing out here now, so pay attention to what you're doing."

They locked eyes for what seemed an eternity.

"Do what I said," Cam told him.

Cam realized too late what Spider was going to do.

In one fluid motion the rogue agent freed the mainsail sheet to allow the boom to swing free, grabbed the helm, put her hard over to leeward and gybed. The gybe is the single most violent action you can take on board a big sailboat in a blow. You put yourself in mortal danger when you turn your bow away from the wind instead of up into it. You stick your tail up into the face of the wind and she kicks your ass. Hard and fast.

The standing rigging and sails shrieked like wounded banshees as the huge mainsail and the heavy wooden boom caught the wind from behind and came whipping across the cockpit at blinding speed.

Spider knew the boom was coming, of course, and ducked in the nick of time. Cam was not so lucky.

The boom slammed into the side of the old man's head, pulverizing the skull, spilling his brains into the sea, and carrying him out of the cockpit and up onto the deck. Only the lifelines saved him from rolling overboard.

Spider stared down at his old mentor with mixed emotions. At one point he'd worshipped this man. But rage is a powerful thing. He'd been ruined by Cam and others like him at the highest levels of the Agency. He knew he himself was going down soon, but he was determined not to go down alone. Revenge is another powerful thing.

He knelt down beside the dead man, trying to sort out his feelings. A lock of white hair had fallen across Cam's eyes and he gently lifted it away. He tried for remorse but couldn't find it inside himself anymore.

It looked like someone had dropped a cantaloupe on the deck from up at the masthead. A dark red stain flowed outward from Hooker's crushed and splintered head, soaking into the teak. What more was there to say? An unfortunate accident but it happens all the time? Tough luck, Cam, he thought to himself with a thin smile.

Another victim of bad timing.

Spider grabbed the helm, sheeted in the main, and headed up dead into the wind. When the boat's forward motion stalled, he grabbed the binoculars hanging from the mizzen and raised them to his eyes. He did a 360-degree sweep of the horizon. Nothing, no other vessels in sight, nobody on the shore. He was about a mile and a half from the shoreline. The trees encroaching down to the rocky shorebreak would provide good cover.

He looked at his watch and went below to don his wet suit for the short swim to shore. The old ketch would drift with the currents. Once back on terra firma, he could disappear into the woods, bury the wet suit, and walk to town in his bathing suit, flip-flops, and T-shirt. Just another hippie tourist day-tripper, come to celebrate America's independence with the Yankee Pilgrims and Puritans.

The next ferry to the mainland was at noon.

He'd checked off yet another name on his list.

Maybe it was true. That the old Spider was indeed a man without a future.

But he still had plenty of time to kill.

CHAPTER 3

TEAKETTLE COTTAGE, ON the south shore of Bermuda, is no ordinary house. For starters, it is the home of the sixth richest man in England, though you'd never guess that from the looks of the place. A small, modest house, it has survived a couple of centuries and at least a dozen hurricanes. And it also happens to be, the sanctum santorum of a very private man. Few people have ever even seen it. To do that, first you'd have to find it.

Anyone searching the Coast Road along the southern shore will find the modest limestone house hidden from view. The seaward property, roughly five acres, consists of a dense grove of banana trees. Also, ancient lignum vitae, kapok, and fragrant cedar trees. Only a narrow and rutted sandy lane gives one a clue as to Teakettle's existence. A drive resembling a green tunnel finally arrives at the house, but only after winding through the densely planted groves.

Upon first glimpse,, you realize the cottage actually does look like a teakettle. The main portion is a rounded dome, formerly a limestone mill works. A crooked white-bricked watchtower on the far, seaward side of the house forms the teakettle's "spout." The whole unassuming affair stands out on a rocky promontory with waves crashing against the coral reefs some fifty feet below.

Inside the dome is an oval whitewashed living room. The floors are highly polished, well-worn Spanish red tile. Wrought iron chandeliers and sconces provide the light. The owner has furnished the main room with old planters chairs and an assortment of cast-offs and gifts donated by various residents seeking their own dream of solitude at the cottage over the last century or so.

Douglas Fairbanks, Jr., one of the cinema's first icons, had donated the massive carved monkey-wood bar after a long, liquid stay when his first wife, Joan Crawford, had thrown him out. Teakettle was a good a place to hide as any. The battered mahogany canasta table where most of the indoor meals were taken was a gift of Errol Flynn. The swashbuckling Flynn took refuge here during his stormy divorce from Lily Damita. Hemingway had left his Underwood typewriter on the guest room desk where he'd completed work on *Islands in the Stream*. It stands there in his honor to this day. The shortwave radio set on the bar had been used by Admiral Sir Donald Gunn during World War II to monitor the comings and goings of Nazi U-boats just offshore from the cottage.

A lot of less celebrated visitors had left behind the detritus of decades, much of which had been severely edited by the new owner. He wasn't a fussy man, but he'd pulled down all the pictures of snakes some prior inhabitant had hung in his small bedroom. He didn't mind disorder as long as it was *his* disorder.

The owner of this rather eccentric dwelling is Lord Alexander Hawke. Hawke won't tolerate your use of his title and has never used it himself. The only one who is allowed to do so is his ancient friend and household retainer, Pelham Grenville, a man whom he has known since birth and is, with the exception of his young son, Alexei, the closest approximation to family he can claim.

Hawke was now a man in his early thirties, a noticeable man, well north of six feet with broad shoulders, a narrow waist, and a heroic head of unruly jet black hair. A thick black comma of hair fell across his forehead despite his best efforts to keep it in check.

His glacial blue eyes (a female friend had once decided they looked like "pools of frozen rain") were startling. His eyes had a flashing range, from merriment and charm to profound earnestness. Cross him, and he could fire a searing flash of blue across an entire room. Hawke had a high, clear brow, and a straight, imperious nose above a well-sculpted mouth with just a hint of cruelty at the corners of a smile.

His job (senior counterintelligence officer at Britain's MI6) demanded that he stay fit. Though he had a weakness for Mr. Gosling's local rum and Morland's custom blend cigarettes, he watched his diet and followed his old Royal Navy fitness regime religiously. He also swam six miles a day in open ocean. Every day.

Attractive, yes, but it was his "What the hell?" grin—a look so freighted with charm that no woman, and even few men could resist—that made him the man he was:

A hale fellow well met, whom men wanted to stand a drink; and whom women much preferred horizontal.

HAWKE HAD BEEN dozing out on the coquina shell terrace that fanned out from doors and windows flung open to the sea on a blue day like this. He had nothing on for today, just supper with his dear friends, the former Chief Inspector of Scotland Yard, Ambrose Congreve, and his fiancée, Lady Diana Mars, at their Bermuda home, Shadowlands, at seven that evening.

"Sorry to disturb you, m'lord," Pelham Grenville said, having shimmered across the sunlit terrace unseen.

"Then don't," Hawke said, deliberately keeping his eyes closed against the fierce sun.

Pelham was the octogenarian valet who'd been in service to the Hawke family in England for decades. When Hawke was but seven years old, he had witnessed his parents' tragic murder by modern day drug pirates aboard their yacht in the Caribbean. Pelham and Chief Inspector Ambrose Congreve had immediately stepped in to raise the devastated child. No one who'd survived that lengthy process would claim that it was easy, but the three men had all remained the closest of friends ever after. Inseparable and insufferable, as they liked to think of themselves these days.

"I think you might wish to take this call, sir," Pelham said.

"Really? Why?"

"It's your friend the Director, m'lord."

"I have many friends who are directors, Pelham. Which one?"

"CIA, sir, he says it's rather important."

"You're joking. Brick Kelly?"

"On the line as we speak, sir."

"Thank you, please tell him I shall be right there."

Hawke had met CIA Director Kelly in an Iraqi prison. Kelly was a U.S. Army spec ops colonel back then, a man who'd been caught red-handed trying to assassinate a Sunni warlord in his mountain village. And Hawke's Royal Navy fighter plane had been shot down over the desert only a few miles from the Iraqi prison. Their treatment was less than five-star; it was no mints on the pillow operation. The guards were inhuman, sadistic, and merciless.

One night, Kelly had been dragged away from their cell. He had looked so broken and weak that Hawke decided he'd not survive another day of malnutrition and torture.

That very night, Hawke planned and managed to effect an escape, killing most of the guards and destroying half the prison in the doing of it. He carried Brick Kelly on his shoulders out into the burning desert. It was four long days before they were rescued by friendlies, both men delirious with hunger, sunstroke, and dehydration. It's the kind of defining experience that brings men of a certain caliber together for the balance of their lives.

He and Brick had been thick as thieves ever since.

Hawke went inside and over to the antique black Bakelite phone sitting atop the far end of the monkey bar. He picked up the receiver.

"Hullo?" he said. By force of habit, he was always noncommittal when answering a phone call.

"Hawke?"

"Brick?"

"It's a secure line, Alex, no worries. I know you're laying low for a while. Well deserved R&R. I called your house number in London to get this one. Sorry to even bother you but something's happened I felt you should know about."

"Trouble?"

"No, not exactly. Sadness is more like it. Alex, your old friend Cameron Hooker died this past weekend."

"Hook died? Was he sick? He never said a word."

"No. It was an accident."

"Ah, hell, Brick. Damn it. What happened?"

"He went for a sail on Sunday morning. Up at his house in Maine. Did it every Sunday of his life apparently. When he wasn't back home by noon, and his wife couldn't reach his cell, Gillian called the sheriff. They found the boat run aground on a small island near Stonington. Hook was aboard, in the stern, dead."

"Heart attack? Stroke?"

"His head was bashed in."

"Foul play?"

"No. He was alone, apparently. At least he was when he left the dock, according to a young fellow hired on for the summer."

"What happened?"

"I don't know much about sailing, Alex. As you well know. Apparently, he attempted some kind of accidental tack in heavy wind and the big wooden boom swung round and hit him in the head."

"A gybe."

"Right, that's the word the boy used. It was blowing pretty good, I suppose. Certainly enough force for something that heavy to kill him. But . . ."

"But what?"

"I hate to even bring this up, Alex. But in the last six weeks a number of other high-level Agency guys of his era have died. Lou Gagosian, Taylor Greene, Max Cohen, and Nicola Peruggia."

"Suspicious deaths? Any of them?"

"No. Not on the surface, anyway. No evidence of foul play at all. It's just the sheer number and timing that's troublesome. And the high number may just be coincidence."

"Or, maybe not."

"Something like that, yeah."

"Want me to look into it?"

"No. Not yet, anyway. All these poor widows and families are in mourning still. And I don't really have any degree of certainty about my suspicions, just my usual extrasensory paranoia."

"But."

"Yeah. But."

"Look here. Hook was a good friend of mine, Brick. If someone killed him, I damn well want to find out who."

"I'm sure you do. I'll tell you what. Let's give it a month or so. See what happens. Anything suspicious crops up, we go full bore. Okay with you?"

"Sure. You know best. When's the funeral? Where?"

"Up at Hook's place, Cranberry Farm, in Maine. Family cemetery on the property. The service is next Friday afternoon at two. North Haven Island. Out in Penobscot Bay east of Camden. If you're going to fly up from Bermuda, there's a private airstrip at the old Tom Watson place."

"I've used it a few times, but thanks."

"That's right, I forgot, you've been out there before. Okay. I'll see you there, then. Sorry, Alex. I know you two guys were close."

"I'm sorry, too, Brick. Last of the old breed. He was a very, very good guy. See you there."

CHAPTER 4

MOST AFTERNOONS, Harding Torrance walked home from work. His cardiac guy had told him walking was the best thing for his heart. He liked walking. Also, he liked walking in Paris. The women, you know? Paris had the world's most beautiful women, full stop, hands down. Plus, his eight-room apartment was on the rue du Faubourg Saint-Honoré. A famous street in one of the fancier arrondisements on the Right Bank.

He'd lived here over twenty years and still didn't know which arrondisement was which. He had learned an expression in French early on and it always served him well in life: "Je ne sais quoi."

I don't know.

His homeward route from the office took him past the Ritz Hotel, Sotheby's, Hermès, Cartier, et cetera, et cetera. You get the picture. Ritzy real estate.

Very ritzy.

Oddly enough, the ritziest hotel on the whole rue was not the one called the Ritz. It was the one called Hotel Le Bristol. What he liked about the Bristol, mainly, was the bar. At the end of the day, good or bad, he liked a quiet cocktail or two in a quiet bar before he went home to his wife. That's all there was to it, been doing it all his life. His personal happy hour.

The Bristol's bar was dimly lit, church quiet, and hidden away off the beaten path. It was basically a nook in a far corner of the lobby where only the cognoscenti, as they say, held sway. Torrance held sway there because he was a big, good-looking guy, always impeccably dressed in Savile Row threads and Charvet shirts of pale pink or blue. He was a big tipper, a friendly guy. Knew the bar staff's names by heart and discreetly handed out envelopes every Christmas.

Sartorial appearances to the contrary, Harding Torrance was one hundred percent red-blooded American. He even worked for the government, had mostly all his life. And he'd done very, very well, thank you. He'd come up the hard way, but he'd come up, all right. His job, though he'd damn well have to kill you if he told you, was Station Chief, CIA, Paris. In other words, Harding was a very big damn deal in anybody's language.

He'd been in Paris since right after 9/11. His buddy from Houston, the new President, had posted him here because the huge Muslim population in Paris presented a lot of high value intel opportunities in one concentrated location. His mandate was to identify the Al Qaeda leadership in France, whisk them away to somewhere nice and quiet for a little enhanced interrogation.

He was good at it, he stuck with it, he got results, and he got promoted, boom, boom, boom. The President even singled him out for recognition in a State of the Union address, had specifically said that he and his team were responsible for saving countless lives on the European continent and in the U.K.

Harding had gone into the family oil business after West Point and a stint with the Rangers out of Fort Bragg. Spec ops duty, two combat tours in Iraq. Next, working for Torrance Oil, he was all over Saudi and Yemen and Oman, running his daddy's fields in the Middle East. But he was no silver spoon boy, far from it. He had started on the rigs right at the bottom rung, working as a ginzel (lower than the lowest worm), working his way up to a floor hand on the kelly driver, and then a bona fide driller in one year.

Oilfields were his introduction to the real world of Islam.

Long story short?

He knew the Muslim mind-set, their language, their body language, their brains, even, knew the whole culture, the warlords, where all the bodies were buried, the whole enchilada. And so, when his pal W needed someone uniquely qualified to transform the CIA's Paris station into a first rate intelligence clearinghouse for all of Europe? Well. Who was he to say? Let history tell the tale.

His competition? Most guys inside the Agency, working in Europe at that time, right after the Twin Towers? Didn't know a burqa from a kumquat, and that's no lie—

CHAPTER 5

"Monsieur Torrance? Monsieur Torrance?"

"Oui?"

"Votre whiskey, monsieur."

"Oh, hey, Maurice. Sorry. Scotch rocks," he said to the head bartender.

"Mais certainment, Monsieur Torrance. *Et, voilà.*"

His drink had come like magic. Had he already ordered that? He knocked it back, ordered another, and relaxed, making small talk, *le bavardage,* with Maurice about the rain, the train bombing in Marseilles. Which horse might win four million euros in the Prix de l'Arc de Triomphe at Longchamp tomorrow. The favorite was an American thoroughbred named Buckpasser. He was a big pony, heralded in the tabloids as the next Secretariat, Maurice told him.

"There will never, ever, be another 'Big Red,' Maurice. Trust me on that one."

"But of course, sir. Who could argue?"

He swiveled on his bar stool, sipping his third or fourth scotch, checking the scenery, admiring his fellow man.

And woman.

Wouldn't you know it? It was a rainy Friday night and he'd told his wife Julia not to expect him for dinner. Something troubling had come up with the state visit of the new Chinese president to the Elysée Palace on Sunday. And something really bad had come up. But . . .

"Sorry, is this seat taken?" she said.

What the hell? He hadn't even seen her come in.

"Not at all, not at all. Here, let me remove my raincoat from the bar stool. How rude of me."

"Thank you."

Très chic, he registered. Very elegant. Blond. Big American girl. Swimmer, maybe, judging by the shoulders. California. Stanford. Maybe UCLA. One of the two. Pink Chanel, head to toe. Big green Hermès Kelly bag, all scruffed up, so loaded. Big rock on her finger, so married. A small wet puffball of a dog and a dripping umbrella so ducked in out of the rain. Ordered a martini, so a veteran. Beautiful eyes and a fabulous body, so a possibility . . .

He bought her another drink. Champagne, this time. Domaine Ott Rose. So she had taste.

"What brings you to Paris, Mrs. . . ."

"I'm Crystal. And you are?"

"Harding."

"Harding. Now that's a good strong name, isn't it? So. Why are we here? Let me see. Oh, yes. Horses. My husband has horses. We're here for the races at Longchamp."

"And that four million euros purse, I'll bet. Maurice here and I were just talking about that. Some payday, huh? Your horse have a shot?"

"I suppose. I don't like horses. I like to shop."

"Attagirl. Sound like my ex. So, where are you from, Crystal?"

"We're from Kentucky. Louisville. You know it?"

"Not really. So, where are you staying?"

"Right upstairs, honey. My hubby took the penthouse for the duration."

"Ah, got it. He's meeting you here, is he?"

"Hardly. Having dinner with his trainer somewhere in the Bois de Boulogne, out near the track, is more like it. The two of them are all juned up about Buckpasser running on a muddy track tomorrow. You ask a lot of questions, don't you, Harding?"

"It's my business."

"Really? What do you do?"

"I'm a writer for a quiz show."

She smiled. "That's funny."

"Old joke."

"You're smart, aren't you, Harding? I like smart men. Are you married?"

"No. Well, yes."

"See? You are funny. May I have another pink champagne?"

Harding twirled his right index finger, signaling the barman for another round. He briefly tried to remember how many scotches he'd had and gave up.

"Cute dog," he said, bending down to pet the pooch, hating how utterly pathetic he sounded. But, hell, he was hooked. Hooked, gaffed, and in the boat. He'd already crawl through a mile of broken glass just to drink this gal's bathwater.

"Thanks," she said, lighting a gold-tipped cigarette with a gold Dupont lighter. She took a deep drag and let it out, coughing a bit.

"So, you enjoy smoking?" Harding said.

"No, I just like coughing."

"Good one. What's the little guy's name?" he asked, looking at the little drowned rat trying to pass for a pooch.

"It's a her. Rikki Nelson."

"Oh. You mean like . . ."

"Right. In the *Ozzie and Harriet* reruns. Only this little bitch on wheels likes her name spelled with two k's. Like Rikki Martinez. Don't you, precious? Yes, you do!"

"Who?"

"The singer?"

"Oh, sure. Who?"

"Never mind, honey. Ain't no thing."

"Right. So, shopping. What else do you like, Crystal?"

"Golf. I'm a scratch golfer. Oh, and jewelry. I really like jewelry."

"Golfer, huh? You heard the joke about Arnold Palmer's ex-wife?"

"No, but I'm going to, I guess."

"So this guy marries Arnold Palmer's ex. After they make love for the third time on their wedding night, the new groom picks up the hotel phone. 'Who are you calling?' Arnie's ex asks. 'Room service,' he says, 'I'm starved.' 'That's not what Arnold would've done,' she says. So the guy says, 'Okay, what would Arnold have done?' 'Arnold would have done it again, that's what.' So they did it again. Then the guy picks up the phone again and she says, 'You calling room service again?' And he says, 'No, baby, I'm calling Arnold. Find out what par is on this damn hole.'"

He waited.

"I don't get it."

"Well, see, he's calling Arnold because he—"

"Sshh," she said, putting her index finger to her lips.

She covered his large hand with her small one and stroked the inside of his palm with her index finger.

She put her face close to his and whispered.

"Frankly? Let's just cut the shit. I like sex, Harding."

"That's funny, I do, too," he said.

"I bet you do, baby. I warn you, though. I'm a big girl, Harding. I am a big girl with big appetites. I wonder. Did you read *Fifty Shades of Grey*?"

"Must have missed that one, sorry. You ever read Mark Twain?"

"No. Who wrote it?"

"Doesn't matter, tell me about *Fifty Shades of Grey*."

"Doesn't matter. I found it terribly vanilla," she said.

"Hmm."

"Yeah, right. That's what men always say when they don't know what the hell a girl is talking about."

"Vanilla. Not kinky enough."

"Not bad, Harding. Know what they used to say about me at my sorority house at UCLA? The Kappa Delts?"

"I do not."

"That Crystal. She's got big hair and big knockers and she likes big sex."

He turned to face her and took both her perfect hands in his.

"I'm sorry. Would you ever in your wildest dreams consider leaving your rich husband and marrying a poor, homeless boy like me?"

"No."

"Had to ask."

"I would, however, consider inviting you upstairs to view my etchings. I like to screw. You do get that part, right?"

"Duly noted."

"Long as we're square on this, Harding."

"We're square."

"I'm gonna tie you to the bed and make you squeal like Porky Pig, son. Or, vice versa. You with me on this?"

He looked at her and smiled.

Jackpot.

CHAPTER 6

THE ELEVATOR TO the Penthouse Suite opened inside the apartment foyer. It was exquisite, just as Harding would have imagined the best rooms in the best hotel in Paris might be, full of soft evening light, with huge arrangements of fresh flowers everywhere, and through the open doors, a large terrace overlooking the lights of Paris and the misty gardens below.

Crystal smiled demurely and led him into the darkened living room. She showed him the bar and told him to help himself. She'd be right back. Slipping into something a little more comfortable, he imagined, smiling to himself as he poured two fingers of Johnnie Walker Blue and strolled over to a large and very inviting sofa by the fireplace.

He kicked his shoes off, stretched out and took a sip of whiskey. He was just getting relaxed when he heard an odd hissing sound. Looking down at the floor he saw that the little fuckhead Rikki Nelson had just peed all over his Guccis.

"Shit!" he said under his breath.

"Hey!" he heard her call out.

"What?"

"Turn on some music, Harding, I want to dance!" she called out from somewhere down a long dark hall.

He got to his feet and staggered a few feet in the gloom, cracking his shin on an invisible marble coffee table.

"What? Music? Where is it?"

"Right below the bar glasses. Just push 'on,' It's all loaded up and ready to rip."

He limped over to the bar and hit the button.

Dean Martin's "That's Amore!" filled the room.

"Is that it?" he shouted over Dino.

"Hell, yeah, son. Crank it!"

He somehow found the volume control, cranked it, and went out to the terrace, away from the bar's booming overhead speakers. The rain was pattering on the drooping awning overhead and the night smelled like . . . like what . . . jasmine? No, that wasn't it. Something, anyway. It definitely smelled like something out here.

"Hey, you!" she shouted from the living room's open doorway. "There he is! There's my big stud. Come on in here, son. Let's dance! Waltz your ass on in here, baby boy, right now!"

He downed his drink and went inside. Crystal stood in the center of the room wearing a skintight black leather bodysuit that would have put the Cat-woman to shame. She had little Rikki Nelson cud-dled in her arms, nuzzling her with kisses.

"Where's the whip?" he said.

"Oh, I'll dig one up somewhere, don't you worry."

Harding collapsed into the nearest armchair and stared.

"Why are you staring like that at me and Rikki?" she pouted.

"Just trying to figure out whether or not that leash is on the wrong bitch."

Give her credit, she laughed.

"I sure hope to hell you know how to dance, mister," she said. "Now get up and get with it, I mean it."

He hauled himself manfully up out of the leather chair.

You do what you have to do, he reminded himself.

And he danced.

And danced some more.

CHAPTER 7

HE WAS DRENCHED in sweat and panting like an old bird dog. Even the sheets were wet. Somehow he'd managed to give her three Big O's, two traditional and, lastly, one utterly exhausting one. He'd never worked so hard in his life. "Outside the box," she called it, that last one.

He managed a weak smile. "Wow, you are something else, aren't you, girl? I need a cigarette."

"No time. Back in the saddle, cowboy. You got me hot now. I'm itching to ride!"

"Crystal, seriously. I need a little breather here."

"Don't be a pussy, Harding. Mama's waiting. Turn over."

"Oh, Christ."

He rolled over onto his back and stared at the ceiling. She took his wrists and tied them to the bedposts with two Hermès scarves she'd plucked from the bed-side table.

He didn't even bother trying to fight her.

"Are you trying to kill me, or what?"

"Don't you worry yourself, baby. The Cialis will kick in any minute now."

"I don't take Cialis, Crystal."

"You do now, stud. I put two in your drink down at the lobby bar. When you bent down to pat Rikki Nelson."

"What? Are you kidding me? F'crissakes, Crys-tal—"

"Don't say I didn't warn you, hon. Big sex, re-member? Okay, I'll get on top this time. Oh, yes . . . somebody's ready for Mama down there. That Cialis is a bitch, isn't it? Just think, two pills, you might have an erection lasting eight hours . . ."

"Listen, Crystal, you've really got to stop this . . . untie me . . . I've got a pain in my chest . . . I mean it!"

"Pussy is the best cure for whatever ails you, son. Hang on, Mama's gonna ride this bucking bronco all the way to the buzzer . . ."

"Damn it, get off! I've got a cardiac condition! Doc says I'm supposed to take it easy . . . Goddam-nit, I'm serious! Now my arm really hurts . . . call the doctor, Crystal. Now. They must have a house doctor on call and. . . . oh, Christ almighty, it hurts . . . do something!"

"Like what?"

"My pills! My nitro pills! They're over there in my trouser pocket . . ."

"Hold on a sec . . ."

She reached over and picked up the bedside phone, never breaking her stride, and asked for the hotel operator.

CHAPTER 8

"My pills! My nitro pills! They're in her other trouser pocket..."

"Hold on a sec."

She reached over and picked up the bedside phone, never bothering to answer the door or the hotel operator.

HE MUST HAVE passed out from the pain. Everything was foggy, out of focus. The room was dark, the rain beating hard against the windowpanes. Just a single lamplight from a table over in the corner.

Crystal, still naked, was sitting with her back to him at the foot of the bed, smoking a cigarette and talking to the doctor in hushed tones. Her head was resting on the doctor's shoulder. He couldn't make out what they were saying. He was bathed in a cold, clammy sweat and the pain had spread from behind his breastbone into and out along his left arm. Fucking hell. His wrists were still tied to the bedposts? Was she insane?

He heard a sob escape his own lips, and then a cry of pain caused by the elephant sitting atop his chest.

"Sshh," the doctor said, getting to his feet and coming to the head of the bed to stand beside him.

He was naked, too. He put his finger to his lips and said "Sshh" again.

"You've gotta do CPR or something, Doc," Harding croaked. "My pills! They're in the right pocket of my trousers. Please. I feel like I'm going to die . . ."

"That's because you are going to die, Harding," the man said.

"What?"

"You heard me."

"Wait. Who are you?" He squinted his eyes but couldn't make out the physician's features.

"Vengeance, sayeth the Lord, Harding. That's who I am. Vengeance."

"You're not a doctor . . . you're . . ."

"Dr. Death will do for now."

"Who . . . no, you're not . . . you're somebody else. You're . . ."

"Don't you recognize me anymore, Harding? I've had a little surgery recently. A bit of Botox. But, still, the eyes are always a dead giveaway. Look close."

"Spider?"

"Bingo."

"No, can't be . . . You're fucking Spider, f'crissakes," the dying man croaked.

"Right. Spider Payne. Your old buddy. Come rain or come shine. Tonight, it's rain. Look out the window, Harding. It's goddamn pouring out there. Ever see it rain so hard?"

"Gimme a break here, Spider. What are you doing . . ."

"It's called poetic justice. A little twist of fate shall we say?"

Pain scorched Torrance's body and he arched upward, straining against his bonds, coming almost completely off the bed. He didn't think anything could hurt this much.

His old nemesis knelt on the floor by the bed and started gently stroking his hair. When he spoke, it was barely above a whisper.

"You fucked me royally, Harding. Remember that? When I needed you most? When the French government, whom you always claimed to have in your pocket, nailed my balls to the wall? Kidnapping and suspicion of murder. Thirty years to life? Ring a bell?"

"That wasn't my fault, f'crissakes! Please! You gotta help me!"

"That's my line. Help me. You don't get to use it. Way too late for that, I'm afraid, old soldier. You're catching the next train, partner."

"I can't . . . I can't breathe . . . I can't catch my . . ."

"This is how it works, Harding."

"What—"

"It's so simple, isn't it? Judgment Day. How it all works out in the end? In that dark hour when no bad deed goes unpunished."

"I can't . . . can't . . ."

Harding Torrance opened his eyes wide in fear and pain. And as the blackness closed in around him he heard Spider Payne utter the last words his addled brain would ever register:

"You fuck me, right? But, in the end, Crystal and the Spider, they fuck you."

CHAPTER 9

A PERFECT DAY for a funeral.

It was raining steadily, but softly. Dripping from the leaves, dripping from the eaves of the old Maine cottage on the hill. Tendrils of misty gray fog curled up from the sea, only to disappear into the steaming pine forests. Thin, ragged clouds scudded by low overhead.

Hook's burial service was in the overgrown family plot. A hallowed patch of small worn gravestones dotting a hilltop clearing overlooking the misty harbor. There were rows and rows of folding white chairs arranged on the grass surrounding the gravesite, filled with mourners hidden beneath rows and rows of gleaming black umbrellas.

There was even a piper in full regalia standing by the freshly opened wound in the rich earth. A white-bearded fellow wearing tartans, an old friend of Hook's who'd rowed over from Vinalhaven for the three o'clock service.

At the center of it all, a yawning grave.

Alex Hawke was seated in the very last row beside his old American friend Brick Kelly. Hawke let his eyes wander where they would, taking it all in, the simple beauty of the rainy day and the still and perfect sadness all around him.

Down at the dock, Hook's black ketch was flying signal flags from stem to masthead to stern, thanks to the young man whom Hawke had just met up at the house. A good-looking college kid Cam Hooker had hired to look after his boat that summer. The boy was sitting a few rows ahead of him with the grand-children now, trying to keep them still.

Hawke had first seen the boy up at the house, trying to catch his eye all morning. Finally, Hawke had said, "Can I help you?"

"You're Lord Hawke, is that correct, sir?" the boy had asked him as they stood together. They were both holding plates, everyone inching forward in the buffet line circling through the living and dining rooms. Both rooms were full of musty old furniture, cracked marine paintings, and frayed rugs made all the more beautiful by age and deliberate lack of care.

"I am, indeed," Hawke said, puzzled. Why should anyone here know who he was? He stood out, he supposed, in his uniform. Royal Navy Blue, No. 1 Dress, no sword. Bit of a spectacle, but nothing for it, it was regulation.

"Ben Sparhawk, sir. I worked for Director Hooker this past summer. Helping out with *Maracaya* and around the dock. I wonder if we might have a word, sir?"

"Of course. What about?"

The fellow looked around and lowered his voice.

"I'd really rather not discuss it here if you don't mind, sir."

Hawke looked at the long line of people slowly snaking toward the buffet tables set up in the dining room. "Let's go out onto the porch and get some air," the Englishman said. "I'm not really hungry anyway."

"Thank you," Ben Sparhawk replied, somewhat shakily. He followed the older man outside into the damp air, misty rain blowing about under the eaves. "I really appreciate your taking the time."

"Something's bothering you, Ben," Hawke said, his hands on the railing, admiring Camden harbor across the bay and the beautiful Maine coastline visible from the hilltop. "Just relax and tell me what it is."

"I don't really know quite where to start and . . ."

It occurred to Hawke that he'd always loved this part of the world. That someday he would very much like to own an old house up here. The late summer air full of white clouds and diving white seabirds, the endlessly waving tops of green forests, the deep rolling swells of the blue sea. Bermuda was lovely; but it wasn't this. For the first time he understood viscerally what his old friend Hook had known and cherished all his life. Down East Maine was closer to Heaven than most places you could name. And you probably couldn't even name one.

"I'm sorry, sir. I don't know the proper form of address I should use. Is it 'Your lordship'?"

"It's Alex, Ben. Just plain old Alex."

The handsome young man smiled. "First of all, I haven't said a word to anyone. About what I'm going to tell you, I mean. But I know who you are and I figured you'd be someone who'd listen. Mr. Hooker talked about you a lot, all the sailing you two had done up here over the years. Northeast Harbor, Nova Scotia, Trans-Atlantic."

"We had some good times," Hawke said, wistful for those fleeting moments, sadly missing his old friend.

"So he often said. Hook always claimed his friend Hawke was the finest blue water sailor he'd ever known, sir. But he was a good sailor, too, wouldn't you say? I was only aboard with him a couple of times out in the bay. But you can tell, right?"

"Absolutely. Hook was a lifelong salt if ever there was one. Still competitive in the Bermuda Race until a few years ago. Why? What is troubling you?"

"Okay. Here goes. There is just no way on earth I can see what happened out there on the water as accidental. None."

"Why?"

"Here's the thing, sir. On the day it happened? Well, it was blowing pretty good out there, all right. Steady at fifteen, gusting to twenty-five, thirty knots.

But nothing Cam Hooker couldn't handle. Had I thought otherwise, I'd have volunteered to go with him. Not that he would have let me, but still."

"Go on."

"I know accidents happen at sea all the time, sir. Hell, I've had my share. But what I cannot understand, what I do not understand, is why on earth Cam Hooker would gybe that big boat, out there all alone, blowing like stink. I'm sure you'd agree that it's the last thing he would do!"

"He gybed the boat? Good Lord. Why the hell would he do that?"

"Beats me, sir. A gybe? It's the dead last thing anyone would do in a blow. Especially someone elderly and sailing single-handed."

"I agree. But what makes you think that's what happened?"

"Okay, here's what I know. I had a few beers down at Nebo's the other night with Jimmy Brown. He's the chief of police here on the island. And he told me that when they found *Maracaya,* she'd drifted awhile and finally run aground on the rocks, out there on Horse Neck Island. The mainsheet, which Cam would have obviously kept cleated, was free. Why? Also, from where Cam was found, the position of the body near the gunwale, it was clear the boom must have knocked him completely out of the cockpit. And he was not a small man, sir."

Hawke nodded his head, seeing it happen.

"That much force could only have resulted from an accidental gybe."

"Yes, sir. And it was no glancing blow, either. His skull, sir, it was . . . almost completely disintegrated."

Ben Sparhawk looked away, his eyes filling up.

"Damn it, sir. I'm sorry. I just . . . I just don't buy it. Accident, human error, Cam's old age, dementia, all that police bull crap. What they're saying in town . . ."

"What do you think really happened, Ben?"

"Maybe I'm crazy, I dunno. But to tell you the truth, murder. I think someone murdered him."

"Murder's a strong word."

"I know, I know. No idea how it happened. No idea why. But you asked me what I think and now you know."

"Take me through it, Ben. Step by step. I'll ask a few questions. Any information you think I need to have, give it to me. Can you do that?"

"Absolutely, sir."

"First. He was alone on board when he left the dock? Is that right?"

"Yes, sir."

"And he sailed out of your sight alone?"

"He did."

"But, once around the point down there, he could have seen a friend on the town docks, or someone on another boat in the harbor could have hailed him over. He could have stopped to let them aboard. A friend along for the ride or something."

"He could have. But—"

"But what?"

"But he just never would have done it. Sunday was his day. He treasured every second he got to spend alone aboard that old boat. He didn't go to church, you know. That boat was his church. His place of refuge. You know what he said to me early on in the summer?"

"I don't."

"He said, 'I discovered something about sailing at a very early age, Ben. Something about the doing of it makes people want to keep their eyes and ears open and their goddamn mouths shut. I like that about it.'"

Hawke smiled. "He hated idle chitchat, all right. Always said they called it small talk for a very good reason."

"Yes, sir. He said sailing all alone had been his salvation as he grew older. That's what I think he believed anyway. I know he had a wonderful family, too. Hell, everyone on this island loved him. Look at them all."

"But you think he would never have stopped to take someone else aboard before he headed for open water."

"Not unless they were drowning"

"Which means the killer, if there was one, had to be hiding aboard when he left the dock last Sunday morning."

"Had to be. Only way."

"But you would have seen someone, hiding aboard, I mean."

"Not really, sir. All I did below that morning was clean up the galley, plug in the espresso machine, check the fuel and water, and turn the battery switches on. Didn't check the bilges, didn't check the sail locker forward. No reason to, really. But, still. I wish to God I had."

"Don't even think of laying this off on yourself, Ben."

"Well. I'm just sayin', is all."

"When did you last check those two places?"

"The afternoon before. One of the bilge pumps needed rewiring and I climbed down there and did that. And I'd bought some new running rigging from Foy Brown's. I stowed it forward in the sail locker until I could get around to it. Nothing in either place, no sign of anyone on board."

"But it had to be a stowaway, Ben. If you're right about all this."

"Yes, sir. It did. But where was he?"

Hawke looked away to the horizon for a moment, thinking it through.

"Assume this is premeditated. He's been watching his victim for some time now. Knows all his habits, his routines."

"Like his weekly Sunday morning sail."

"Exactly. So. Saturday night, early Sunday morning. Our stowaway comes aboard in the wee hours, when everyone's asleep. Finds the boat unlocked, so he goes below. Finds room enough to hide in the sail locker up at the bow. Sleeps up forward on top of the sails and prays no one needs a reason to open that hatch before she next left the dock."

"That would work."

"Comes up on deck after she clears the harbor. Confronts his victim. Has a gun or a knife. Words are exchanged. Sees how hard it's blowing. Sees the opportunity for an 'accidental' gybe. No one is around to see. He realizes on the spot that he can make the murder look like an accident."

Ben nodded in the affirmative. "Maybe Cam knows him. Maybe not afraid of him. The killer stands there talking in the cockpit, making Cam relax, let his guard down. Then he suddenly frees the mainsheet and puts the helm hard over. Wham! She gybes! Cam never saw that boom coming at him."

"Was there brain tissue found on the boom, Ben?"

"Yes, sir, I think there was. I heard a cop say so, but I couldn't look."

"Then what happens?"

"Looks around. Makes sure he hasn't been seen, I guess. Leaves Cam lying there like that. Maybe dead, maybe still alive. But not for long. He uncleats the mainsheet, the jib sheet, let's her drift with the currents."

"How does he get off the boat? Water's freezing."

"Has a wet suit stowed up in the sail locker and swims ashore?" Ben said.

"Exactly. Are you thinking a native of North Haven? Cam have any enemies at all on this island, Ben? By that I mean serious enemies."

"No, sir. He did not. Had a few run-ins with plumbers and caretakers, the usual disagreements over money or the quality of work over the years. But, as I say, most everybody who knew him, loved him. And nobody hated him. I would have known. Everybody knows everything around here, believe me."

"So he comes over from the mainland by boat the day before. Late Saturday night, let's say. His own boat, maybe, or a rental, or stolen in Camden harbor. Something to check out with your friends at the local constabulary. Sails over to North Haven from Rockport or Camden. Hides his skiff somewhere along the shore for the night. Hikes out here to Cranberry Point sometime after midnight and climbs aboard the ketch. Tucks in for the night. Main hatch leading below was not locked I'd assume."

"Never. There's one other option. He takes the ferry from Rockland the afternoon before. Brings his car aboard. Or, leaves it at the mainland ferry station. Either way."

"You're right. We've established opportunity. So, all we need is a motive."

"I reckon you'd know a lot more than me about that kind of thing, sir."

"I reckon I would, Ben. If I don't, CIA Director Brick Kelly sure does. Thank you for coming to me. It was the right thing to do. Does Cam's wife know anything about your suspicions?"

"No, sir, she doesn't. I would never have said anything about what might still be a whole lot of nothin'.

You are the one and only person I've talked to about this."

"I may need your help here on the island, Ben. I'll talk to the Director after the funeral."

"Anything at all. I loved the old guy, sir. I'm pretty sure you did, too."

"Look, Ben, I'm flying back to Bermuda first thing tomorrow morning. But if Brick Kelly and I both conclude that you're onto something here, I'd like you to stick around here on North Haven as long as you can. Just in case we have any follow-up questions for the police chief or other things we'd like you to look into around here. When do you have to be back at New Haven?"

"I've got a few weeks left before fall term starts, sir."

"Good. I'll talk to Director Kelly tonight. If he concurs, you're working for the CIA now, Mr. Sparhawk. Just temporarily, of course."

"Yes, sir!" Ben Sparhawk said with a smile. For a second Hawke was afraid he was going to salute.

"Don't get too excited, Ben, you don't get the secret decoder ring just yet."

CHAPTER 10

AFTER THE SERVICE, Hawke told Brick Kelly they needed to talk. Something that couldn't wait until next morning. At first light, Hawke was giving the Director a lift down to Washington in his plane. He would drop him off at Andrews Air Force Base before heading out over the Atlantic to his beloved getaway cottage on Bermuda.

That evening, after the funeral, the two old friends strolled down into town from the Hooker place. Gillian had been kind enough to put them up for the night, in two tiny bedrooms up on the third floor, and they'd enjoyed spending the extra time together.

They were quiet, admiring the lights coming on in the little village of North Haven, and the old boatyards and the casino before climbing the hill to the Nebo Lodge. The inn overlooked the sailboats swinging on their moorings in the tranquil harbor.

Nebo was the only restaurant on the island, and it was a damn fine one by Hawke's lights.

They ate in the bar. It was packed with mourners drowning their sorrows. Hawke had once asked an old islander why folks seemed to drink a lot around here. "Because, boy, there ain't nothing to do and we spend all our time doing it" was the fellow's response. Every face Hawke saw there that night he'd seen earlier at Hook's funeral. No one paid the slightest mind to the two off-islanders talking quietly at a corner table. Hawke had discreetly given the hostess a substantial gratuity to ensure no one was seated near them.

Their drinks came and Brick solemnly raised his glass of amber whiskey.

"To Hook," the Virginian said. "None finer, and many a damn sight worse."

"We loved you, Hooker," Hawke said simply, and downed his rum.

"We sure as hell did," Brick said, and signaled the waitress for another round.

He looked at Hawke, glad of his company. It had been far too long since they'd been able to spend a quiet evening together in a place like this. Something they used to do all the time. Just bullshit and drink. Small talk would come later, they had business to discuss first.

The tall and lanky Virginian settled back in his chair toward the window, his red hair aflame in the sunset's last rays, his sea-blue eyes alight. Brick had always had an old-fashioned, almost Jeffersonian air about him; he even looked a good deal like young Tom Jefferson in the prime of his life. He looked at Hawke and smiled.

"Well, old buddy? You said you had something to tell me," Brick said.

"I do," Hawke said, "And you said you had something you wanted to tell me. You first."

Brick Kelly laughed.

"All right, Hawke, that's how you want to be. There was a message waiting for me up in my dorm room after the funeral. The deputy director at Langley. Are you listening?"

"Fire when ready."

"Okay. My guy. CIA Chief of Station, Paris? You know him?"

"Nope."

"Guy named Harding Torrance. A lifer. Old friend of the Houston oil crowd, Bush forty-one appointee."

"I remember him now, yeah. Big, strapping fellow. Real cowboy, as I recall."

"Yeah, well, the real cowboy's real dead."

Hawke sat forward.

"Another one? Tell me what happened, Brick."

"Died with his boots on, apparently. In bed in a suite at the Hotel Bristol in Paris. This was . . . what . . . roughly six hours ago now. Harding was with a woman, married, whom he'd just met in the hotel bar. Her room, she was a registered guest. All legit. You should know that this was not unusual behavior on his part. Torrance considered himself quite the swordsman. Neither here nor there, he never let it interfere with his work."

"Meaning?"

"Meaning he saved a whole lot of innocent lives in the aftermath of 9/11. That gets him a bit of a pass in my book."

"Cause of death?"

"Coronary. Big-time. Massive. Happened in the sack. According to his newly acquired inamorata, Mrs. Crystal Saxby of Louisville, Kentucky, they were having sex when the event occurred. She says she immediately called for a house doctor and administered CPR while she was waiting, but it was too late. He was gone by the time anyone got there."

"So sad when love goes wrong," Hawke said, sipping his rum.

Brick smiled.

"Yeah. Apparently the husband walked in while she was still nude. Sitting on his chest and attempting mouth-to-mouth, but that's only hearsay. One of my guys on the scene provided that picturesque grace note."

"What do you think, Brick? Foul play?"

"Tell you this. The gendarmes and the Paris M.E. guys have already called it. Natural causes."

"No sign of succinylcholine in his bloodstream? Or, that new heart attack dart?"

"I ordered my own autopsy. Nada on the drugs,

so far. No denatured poisons, and no sign of a dart entry."

"The heart dart leaves a mark? I didn't know that."

"Yeah, a tiny red dot on the skin. Easy to miss. Goes away quickly, though."

"So? Clean?"

"Yeah, maybe. I still don't like the timing, but yeah, I suppose he just had a heart attack brought on by excessive sexual exertion. Happens all the time. I guess."

"You guess? You never guess. What's wrong, Brick? Tell me what you really think."

"Hell, I don't know, Alex. Maybe nothing. Maybe it is what it is. But a couple of troublesome details. My guys found heart meds in his pants pocket. Little silver heart-shaped pillbox from Tiffany, monogrammed. So. This coronary was no surprise attack. Nitro pills and beta-blockers in his pocket? We checked. He's under the care of the top cardiac specialist in Paris. He feels a heart attack coming on, first thing he does, he tells the woman to call his doctor and to go get him his damn meds, right? Like, right now?"

"Anybody ask the woman that question?"

"They will tomorrow morning. I'm having her brought back in to the Prefecture for another interview. So, anyway. Who the hell knows? That's my latest tale of mayhem and mystery. Let's order some dinner and you tell me yours."

Hawke took ten minutes and told Kelly everything Ben Sparhawk had said about Cam Hooker's death while they waited for their food.

"What are you thinking?" Hawke asked Brick after a few minutes of contemplative silence from his friend.

"Question," Brick said.

"Go."

"Let's be realistic here. Could someone commit a fairly sophisticated murder here in Maine on Sunday and then pull off another one four days later in Paris? Even more elaborate?" I mean, seriously. Who the hell is good enough to pull that off?"

"Cam was a pretty tough act to follow, all right."

Hawke waited a beat and said, "Maybe we've got it all wrong. Can you connect any of these dots, Brick? Between these two most recent guys and the other ones? Because I'm telling you right now that if we can't . . . well . . . mere coincidence starts to look pretty good again."

Brick took a bite of his steak and said, "Don't go there yet. Stay open to it. But I hear you. I'm on the connect-the-dots issue as soon as I get back to my office tomorrow. I'll call your Bermuda number if and when I get any positive hits. Correlations, I mean."

CHAPTER 11

THE RAIN HAD STOPPED.

After dinner at Nebo, Hawke and Brick walked back to the Hooker place, taking the main road along the harbor. It was a full moon, hanging bright and white and big in the sky. Each man knew what the other was thinking. There was no need of talking about it.

Finally, as they turned into the long Hooker drive, Brick stopped and looked at his friend.

"What's your gut telling you, Alex?" Brick said. "Right this minute. Don't edit. Spit it out."

"Okay. That the timing of all this no coincidence. That what you've got is a totally bad-ass rogue agent running around the planet systematically killing your own top guys."

"Yeah. That's where I come out, too."

"Let me find him for you, Brick."

"Are you kidding? It's my problem, not yours. My agency. My people getting killed. God knows, MI6 has got enough of its own problems these days. That intel meltdown in Syria, for starters."

"This guy, whoever he is, killed my friend Hook, Brick. That makes him my problem, too."

"You're serious. You want to take this on?"

"I do."

"You even have time to do this?"

"I've got another two weeks before C wants me to mysteriously appear in a Damascus souk, looking to purchase some bargain-basement Sarin gas."

Brick looked at him and they started climbing the hill.

"Two weeks isn't a long time to find a seasoned operative who's gone to ground without a trace. Now roaming the globe on a murder spree but not leaving any tracks. But, listen, Alex. Hell, I won't stop you from looking. Nobody is better at this than you. Just tell me what you need."

"Don't worry, I will. This is obviously not an MI6 operation. You're right. And C and the brass at MI6 will pitch a fit if they find out I've gone freelance. So, I need somebody attached to this op at Langley. Files on every possible disaffected agent who had ties to multiple victims, for starters. Active and inactive. Send everything to Bermuda. I'll get Ambrose Congreve on this with me. He's there at his home on Bermuda now, as luck would have it."

"Your very own 'Weapon of Mass Deduction.'. If he can't solve this, no one can."

"Exactly."

"I'll tell you one thing," Brick said, never breaking his stride but taking a deep breath and staring up at the blazing moon and cold stars. "I'm really going to miss Hook, that old bastard, won't you, Alex?"

"I sure as hell will. But I'll feel a whole lot better when I catch the son of a bitch who bloody killed him, I can tell you that bloody much. It won't be pretty."

"Easy," he said, "Easy there, old compadre."

"Who the hell, I ask you, who the hell would ever want to murder a fine old Yankee gentleman like Hook?"

"Go find out, Alex. Whoever he is, he needs killing soon. I have a lot of justifiably nervous campers out there right now."

"Yeah. Murder's bad for institutional morale."

"Ambrose will have every shred of evidence I can pull together arrive at his Bermuda address by courier within forty-eight hours."

"Sooner the better. A couple of weeks isn't a long time."

CHAPTER 12

It didn't take Ambrose that long.

"Sorry to disturb you, sir," Pelham said.

"Not at all, Pelham."

"Chief Inspector Ambrose Congreve here to see you, sir," Pelham said, wafting farther out into the sunshine-spattered terrace. "A matter of some urgency, apparently."

It was a brilliant blue Bermuda day, but embankments of purple cloud were stacking up out over the Atlantic. Storm front moving due east. Hawke put down the book he was reading, a wonderful novel called *The Sea,* by John Banville. It made him want to read every word the man had ever written.

"Thank you, Pelham. Won't you show him out?"

"Indeed, I shall, m'lord."

"Offer him a bit of refreshment, will you, please?"

"But of course, your lordship."

Pelham withdrew soundlessly back into the shadows of the house.

Hawke smiled as he watched the old fellow retreat. These stilted conversational formalities had not been necessary for years. But it was something Hawke and his octogenarian friend Pelham Grenville found so amusing they continued the charade. Both men found an odd reassurance in these hoary, Victorian exchanges. It was a code they shared; and the fact that an outside observer would find them old-fashioned and ridiculous made their secret all the more enjoyable.

Moments later Ambrose Congreve walked out onto the terrace at Teakettle Cottage with a big smile on his face. He was wearing a three-piece white linen suit with a navy blue bow tie knotted at his neck and a white straw hat on his head, something Tennessee Williams might have conjured up. He was even dabbing at his forehead with a white linen handkerchief as Big Daddy might have done.

Congreve had been busy. He had spent the last two days in his home office at Shadowlands, sifting through mobile intercepts, old dossiers, photographs, all the reams of highly classified material Brick Kelly had forwarded out from Langley. And, judging by appearances this morning, the famous criminalist had come up with the goods.

"Oh, hullo, Ambrose," Hawke said, raising his sunglasses onto his forehead. "Why are you in such a fiendishly good mood this morning?"

"Does it show?"

"You look like you've been sitting in a corner eating canaries all morning."

Congreve waved the comment away and sat down on the nearest rattan chair. He carried a lot of excess weight and was always glad of a place to sit.

"Alex, pay attention. This is serious. You don't by any chance know someone, a former high-ranking CIA officer, by the name of Artemis Payne, do you?"

Hawke looked up.

"Who did you say?"

"Payne. Artemis Payne."

"You're joking."

"I assure you that I am not, Alex, joking."

Hawke scratched his chin, realizing he'd forgotten to shave. Bermuda did that to you.

"We called him Spider-Man," he said. "Or, to his face, just plain Spider. No idea where it came from. But it fit. A rather venomous creature to be honest."

"Tell me about him."

"Spider Payne. I know him all right. I worked with him a couple of times in the past. The Caribbean. But Africa, mostly. A deeply troubled man. Why?"

"He might be your chap, Alex. You can draw straight lines through the late Steven Dedalus, CIA head in Dublin, to Cam Hooker at Langley, and now Harding Torrance in Paris, and they all intersect in the same place. The doorstep of one Artemis Payne. He's your man, all right. I'd bet the farm on it. Not the whole CIA "Farm" of course, just my own little lean-to shed down in Lynchburg."

"Apart from the CIA intersections, is there any other evidence that makes you think Artemis is our guy?"

Ambrose got to his feet, laced his fingers behind his back and began pacing back and forth. A little affectation he'd picked up from his idol, the incandescent Sherlock Holmes, Hawke had always assumed. "Are you quite ready?" Ambrose said.

"Quite."

"Artemis Payne, widely known in the press at the time of his trial as the Spider Man. Currently wanted for kidnapping and suspicion of murder by the French government. Interpol has a standing warrant for his arrest for murder. He received a thirty-year sentence in French courts and skipped. Disappeared completely."

"What triggered all this?" Hawke asked.

"A CIA rendition op gone bad, apparently. Don't forget, this was all shortly after 9/11. A French citizen, a shopkeeper believed by Payne to be an Al Qaeda commander, was kidnapped off a Paris street and never seen again by his wife and family. The French police went after Payne for it. Arrested and convicted. He appealed to Washington and the CIA for help. The White House disavowed his existence. So did CIA. Payne was politically inconvenient. Hung out to dry. There's your motive, obviously."

"Yes."

"Payne lost everything in the aftermath of the trial. His reputation, his house, family, money, the lot of it. He went underground. Nobody's seen him since."

"Hmm."

"Is that really all you have to say? Just 'hmm'? After the mountains of intel I've been sifting through this last week?"

"Oh, do sit down and relax. I know you're wound up about this but it's bad for your nerves to be so excitable."

"Alex, if you think I drove all the way out here to be—"

Hawke looked up, his blue eyes suddenly gone dead serious as the reality of Ambrose's news sank in. He said: "Spider is extraordinarily dangerous. In a bad way, I mean."

"There's a good way?"

"Yeah. People like me. And even you."

Ambrose sat back on the planters chair and accepted another frosty iced tea delivered by Pelham on a silver tray.

"Will that be all, sir?" Pelham asked Hawke.

"Thank you, Pelham, yes. Most kind."

Congreve watched this formal exchange with a smile of bemused indulgence and said, "We've now got precisely one week. We're going to need a lot of help to find this character, Alex. No trail at all. He went from Europe to Miami to Costa Rica where two paths diverge in a wood. Then it all goes stone cold.

We're going to need formidable manpower and time to track his movements and see where it all leads so—"

"Not necessarily."

"Why not? What are you thinking?"

"NSA tracks all these guys who go rogue. Emails, texts, mobile calls, obviously. All I need is a number for him. Everyone has a number, no matter where they're hiding."

"Then what?"

"I call him up. Out of the blue. Long time, no see, Spider. What are you up to these days? Doing well?"

"Alex, please. Don't be ridiculous. You don't think that will arouse suspicion? He knows you have close ties to CIA at the highest levels. He'll be waiting for you, poised to sting."

"I want him to be suspicious. Listen. He compromised my position once. Morocco. Long time ago. I was working out of La Mamounia, running a former Al Qaeda warlord for months, had him buying Stinger missiles at the underground arms bazaar for me. Spider, who always owed the wrong people a lot of money, got offered a tidy sum for my name and he gave me up. Almost got me killed, that nasty bastard. I went after him with a vengeance. Found him hiding in some hellish rathole or other in Tangiers. Locked myself inside with him for two days. Came as close to turning out his lights as I could without pulling the plug, believe me. Told him if I ever saw his face again, I bloody well would kill him."

"He's afraid of you."

Hawke laughed.

"Oh, I'd say so. Yes. I'd say Artemis Payne is very definitely afraid of me."

"Then follow the logic, Alex. As soon as he knows you're looking for him, he'll run. He'll dive deep. Or, worse, he'll lay a trap for you."

"I don't think so. You don't know him like I do. I think as soon as he believes I'm looking for him, he'll come looking for me. That's what any smart guy like Spider would do. You don't sit around and wait, you don't spend the rest of your life looking over your shoulder. No. You go on offense. Eliminate the threat. It's smart. That's what I'd do, too."

"You want him to come here? To Bermuda?"

"I do. And, believe me, he will."

"Then what?"

"I have no earthly idea. I'm no bloody fortune-teller."

"What?"

"I have to make it up, Ambrose."

"There is that, I suppose."

"Right. And you have to help me because this guy is good. And he's not only smart, he's a vicious killer, and he's utterly ruthless. And, to make matters worse, at this point he's got absolutely nothing left to lose."

"I wonder. Have you been experiencing any suicidal thoughts lately, Alex?"

"Please, Constable, don't be ridiculous. Many

people have tried to kill me over the course of my career, and more often than not I've managed to show them the folly of that ambition."

Congreve uttered one of his trademark sighs of exasperation.

"All right, then. What do you need, Alex? I mean, right now?"

"I'll need people watching the airport round the clock, people who know what he looks like. Get a likeness from CIA. Also, same setup at the steamship docks in Hamilton and out at the Royal Navy Dockyards where the cruise ships land. I want to know the second the Spider man sets foot on this island."

"Done. What else?"

"Your brain, if you're not using it at the moment. We need to figure out every last detail of where and how this little reunion should occur."

Congreve said, "Do it here."

"What?"

"Right here at Teakettle Cottage. Gives you the advantage."

"Why?"

"Your own turf, that's why. You cannot arrange something like this, Alex. You've got to sit tight and let the fly come to the spider, as it were."

Hawke laughed at that.

"As opposed to the spider coming to the fly. Who also happens to be a spider."

"Don't be rude, Alex, you know I'm only using a rough analogy. I can't help it if his bloody name is Spider, can I? Stop kidding around and pay attention. Your bloody life is at stake here. This cottage is where he will come looking for you. And this is where you should be waiting."

"I agree, I suppose. But I don't want Pelham in the house or anywhere near me until this tempest in a teakettle is over. Can he stay with you and Diana for a few days? Until this blows over?"

"Of course. I've a lovely guest room for him at Shadowlands, top floor, right on the sea."

"Perfect. Spoil him rotten, will you? He deserves it, God knows."

"We'd like nothing better. Now, what else?"

"I'd like the airport and cruise ship spotters to report to you, not me. As soon as he lands, they alert you. Then you keep track of his movements until he is about to arrive at my doorstep. Just call my house phone, let it ring three times and hang up. Spider's not the type to lob a bomb down the chimney and hope it explodes. He'll want a confrontation. He'll want to talk. He'll want all the drama. Show me how fearless and brilliant he is before he pulls a knife or a gun. That's his style. One of those fellows who always thinks he's the smartest, most dangerous man in the room."

"You do realize, Alex, that if we've even slightly miscalculated, and this man does manage to kill you, that it is my rather prominent posterior that will be in a wringer with C?"

"I've considered it. Sir David will be extraordinarily pissed off with you. It won't be pleasant. Your life won't be worth living. Please accept my abject apologies in advance."

"You'll need a gun, I daresay."

Hawke smiled.

"You know what my American pal Stokely Jones, Jr. always says when someone tells him something as obvious as that?"

"I do not."

"I am a gun."

CHAPTER 13

THE PHONE RANG.

Once. Twice. Three times.

Hawke waited.

It did not ring again.

Game on.

Hawke, seated in his armchair facing the door, closed his eyes and concentrated on sensory input. He listened intently, heard nothing amiss. He rested his chin in one hand, periodically sipping his cold coffee and staring into the pitch-black night beyond his windows. The crackling fire he'd lit earlier now provided barely enough heat to reach his bones.

The minutes crawled by. Interminable . . . He fantasized briefly about a short rum and a cigarette but forced himself to concentrate. See, hear, smell, feel . . .

Some fluting bird call in the night startled him

awake. He sat forward and looked over at the old
station clock hung crookedly above the bar. Three
hours had somehow passed. It was almost midnight.

Bloody hell. He must have dozed off, despite all
the coffee. The log fire had long gone out and the
room felt damp and bone cold. He could see white
plumes of warm breath when he exhaled. Beyond his
walls, the weather was deteriorating.

The wind was up. Shrieking under the eaves and
down the chimney. On the seaward side of the house
he could hear the muffled echo of the rolling sea
booming on the rocks far below.

That cold front he'd seen had moved in over the
island after sunset; now it seemed like it had been raining all evening. The temperature had plummeted and
palm fronds and banana leaves rustled and scratched
against the windows. All the old wooden shutters had
been made fast against the approaching storm. And
any random intruder.

There was only one visible way inside, and that
was through the front door.

He sat forward once more, listening.

He had heard another kind of noise this time, low
and distant. An automobile, its tires hissing on the
rain-wet tarmac ribbon of the coast road. He got
up from his chair facing the front door. He moved
quickly from one to another of the northern expo-
sure windows, all facing the solid wall of banana
trees and the coast road beyond the groves.

Turn left out of his drive and you would eventually

wind your way along the coast and reach the Royal Navy Dockyards. Turn right and you had a half hour's drive until you reached the Bermuda airport. The car seemed to be approaching from the right.

The sound of hissing tires on asphalt suddenly ended. The driver had turned off the main road and onto the sandy lane that led to Hawke's door.

Peering out into the darkness of the groves, he could see distant flashes, hazy arrows of light in the rain-drenched night. The flashes soon resolved into steady twin beams of yellowish illumination. Periodically, they would flare up and spike the blackness deep within the impenetrable banana groves. He could see the dense trees out there, their broad green leaves waving wet and storm-tossed like the sea.

He was on full alert now.

The wavering headlamp beams would disappear for a few seconds, and then reappear after a few seconds closer still, meandering through the groves, stabbing through the trees as if reaching out for him.

Each time a little closer to his cottage . . .

. . . came the spider to the fly.

But the fly had no fear.

Moments like these were what Alex Hawke had lived and breathed for all his life. He was naturally good at war. His father had always said that he was a boy born with a heart for any fate. And the fate he'd been born for was war. He felt the reassuring weight of his weapon on his right side. A big six-shot revolver, the most reliable weapon in his limited arsenal here on Bermuda.

He was wearing loose-fitting black Kunjo pants from Korea. Strapped to his right thigh was a .357 Colt Python revolver in a nylon swivel holster. It was his "Dirty Harry Special": the six-inch barrel, with six magnum parabellum rounds loaded in the cylinder. He wore a black Royal Navy woolen jumper, four sizes too big. It came almost to his knees, giving him freedom of movement and concealing his weapon. He'd cut a hole in the right side pocket so he could keep his hand on his gun without it being seen.

He was barefoot despite the cold tiles beneath his feet . . .

Hawke padded silently across the dark room, returning to the wooden armchair facing the door. He sat down and waited. He looked at the clock again. Only eight minutes had passed since Ambrose called him with the agreed upon signal. Time was elongated, stretching every minute into two or three . . .

A sudden flash of light stretched across the ceiling.

Outside, he heard the automobile roll to a stop some twenty or thirty feet from the entrance.

Automobile tires made a loud crunching sound on the crushed shell drive leading up to Teakettle Cottage. A primitive alarm system, perhaps, but it worked. He jumped up and went to the window again, pulling back the curtain just as the headlamps were extinguished.

A black sedan, undistinguished, a cheap rental from the airport.

Hello, Spider.

Because of the car's misty, rain-spattered windows, he couldn't see inside the vehicle. Only the dark silhouette of a large man behind the wheel. He waited for the car's interior lights to illuminate. It remained dark inside. There was no movement at all from the driver and the four doors remained closed.

He went back to his chair, sat, and waited in the dark for a knock on the heavy cedar door.

It didn't come.

The wind had suddenly died down. The cottage was stone silent save for the ticking of the clock above the bar. No noise or movement inside, nor any noise or movement outside. He tried to imagine what Spider might be doing out there. Just sitting in his car, trying to smoke out his prey? Or trying, somewhat successfully, to psyche his opponent out?

Enough of this, he thought, reaching for his weapon. He'd go outside and confront the man there.

He was about to get out of his chair when his thick wooden front door was suddenly blown inward and off its hinges by a thunderous explosion, a blast of sound and light sufficiently powerful that it blinded him momentarily and disoriented him. His chair was knocked backward and he hit the floor hard after upending a very solid oak table.

He was just vaguely aware that his heavy front

door was hurtling through space directly toward him when it crashed against the wall behind him, a few feet above his head, and splintered into vicious flying spikes.

He got to his feet, shaking his head to clear it. He was shaken, perhaps, but seemingly unscathed. The room was full of smoke and whirling debris; javelin sharp splinters of wood littered the floor.

"Hello, Hawke," a rumbling voice from within the clouds of smoke said.

The man was suddenly standing in the doorway, filling the frame. Hawke would have known that voice anywhere. Gravelly, edgy, and deep, meant to intimidate. Hawke looked down at his clothes, casually dusting himself off with the back of his hand.

"Next time, try knocking, Spider," Hawke said with a thin smile.

"Right. I'll try and remember that."

All in black, Payne was wearing full night combat fatigues, even a helmet with night vision goggles. He had an M4A1 assault rifle slung from his shoulder and what looked like a Sig Sauer 9mm sidearm on his hip. Someone he knew on this island had access to the good stuff. And had provided the assassin with full-bore weapons and gear. Clearly, this was not a social call.

"But then again," Spider added, "there won't be any next time for you and me, old buddy." He took a few steps forward into the room.

"No, I don't suppose that there will be," Hawke said, righting his chair. "I'd invite you in, but you're already in."

Hawke realized his voice showed a lot more confidence than he was feeling right now. He was seriously disadvantaged, clearly having made the old mistake of bringing a metaphorical knife to a legitimate gunfight. Definitely outgunned here, the big Python suddenly feeling more like a peashooter. His mind went into overdrive. He needed a new plan. Somehow, he had to remove himself from this confrontation and hit the reset button.

Had to keep him talking. Right now Hawke was in mortal danger, and both men knew it.

"Sorry about your old buddy Hook," Payne said, "I figured I might hear from you when you heard about the old man's accident."

"The accident."

"Yeah, well."

"So you came here to kill me, too. You think I threw you under the bus for that fiasco in Paris? Nothing to do with it, Spider. I think you got a raw deal. We all did. Everything you did was by the book. Strictly legal operation. I know a lot of other agents who are still pissed at the way you were treated. I'm on your side."

"Save it, Alex. I was on North Haven. I went back for the funeral just to see what I could see. What I saw is you and your bosom buddy Brick Kelly huddled up at a back table at the Nebo Lodge. Didn't take much to figure out what you were talking about. Then I get a phone call from you out of the blue. That's why I'm here, Lord Hawke. Preemptive strike. You know the drill."

"Really? Going to be tough to make this one look accidental, Spider, my bloody door blown off the hinges and all . . ."

Hawke had both hands in his pockets under the cover of his sweater. He surreptitiously moved his right hand to the Colt Python's grips. He carefully swiveled the holster upward . . . easing the hammer back to the cocked position . . . finger applying light pressure to the trigger . . . all without Spider seeing a thing.

"I don't give a shit anymore, Alex. Kelly will have the whole goddamn CIA on my ass now. But I plan to stay alive as long as I can. And take as many of those Agency assholes with me as I can. You understand that kind of thinking, right? Hell, I can see you doing the same damn thing if you got screwed by MI6 the way I did by CIA. Tell me you wouldn't, because I know—"

Hawke fired twice, right through the bulky sweater.

The heavy mag rounds caught Payne high on his right side. He spun around in a mad pirouette and staggered backward through the doorway and into the rain. At the same time, he brought up the muzzle of his automatic weapon and squeezed off a long burst, the staccato rattle deafening inside the small cottage, bullets spraying everywhere.

Hawke dove behind the upended table. The high-powered rounds splintered bits and chunks of wood

all around him. Couldn't remain here a second longer
. . . his cover was disintegrating before his eyes.

He popped up and fired again.

He missed high and left, but caused Spider to
duck down, move sideways on the front steps and
take cover outside behind the exterior wall.

Hawke turned and bolted down the hallway leading to the seaward part of the house, toward his bedroom. Despite all the warning signs, he'd seriously
underestimated his enemy. Cocky, that was the only
word for his stupid behavior.. And that's precisely
how you got yourself killed in this business.

He needed a few precious seconds to think his
way out of that very likely scenario.

CHAPTER 14

HAWKE DASHED INSIDE his room.

Spider was right on his heels, pounding down the long hallway after him.

Inside the small bedroom, Hawke whirled around and slammed the heavy wooden door behind him. He double-bolted it and then slid his large mahogany dresser in front of it, thinking about how this could play out, trying to see it in his mind.

Spider had come prepared for all-out war. He was wearing ceramic body armor plates inside his combat jumpsuit. In order to survive, Hawke had to put a round between one of the seams between the armor plates . . . and hope to hit a vital organ.

And how the hell did you do that staring down the barrel of a roaring machine gun throwing lead at you? He looked around the room, trying to subdue the panic that was creeping around the edges on his

conscious mind . . . A weapon? Some way out of this
. . . had to be!

He spotted one of Pelham's round needlepoint
rugs in the center of the bedroom floor.

There might be a way . . .

His bedroom was directly above the sea. A long
time ago he'd had the crazy notion of installing a
fireman's pole beneath his bedroom floor. His initial
idea had been to use it to slide down the twenty or
thirty feet to the narrow lagoon that lay just beneath
his room. He'd envisioned it as a great way to wake
up each morning. Slide naked from his bed, grab the
pole, and wake up in the clear cold seawater. The
novelty had soon worn off. . . . but the pole was still
there!

He stepped to the center of his small room. Lifted
up the circular rug with a sailboat on it. Beneath it
was the round hatch he'd disguised to match the rest
of the wooden flooring. Never thinking he'd need an
escape hatch but just have it, a secret like a bookcase
that swung open to reveal a hidden passage.

He hooked his finger under an edge and lifted.

Spider was hammering on the door with his fist,
kicking it hard with his heavy boots. Telling Hawke
it was over, useless, time to die. It would be the work
of a few moments before the powerful brute gained
entry.

Yes! Twenty feet directly below Hawke's room
lay the small enclosed lagoon that opened out to the
open sea. He could see the gleaming pole disappear-

ing into the dark waves below, frothing up against the steep rocky walls.

Angered, Spider was firing his weapon at the door, splintering the timbers. Hawke knew he didn't have long—

He jumped, grabbed the pole and slid down, lowering himself just a couple of feet. Then he reached up and pulled the hatch cover with its attached rug back into place. Even if Spider got inside the room now, well, he'd just bought himself a little time . . . a minute, maybe . . .

Go!

He let go of the hatch cover and let himself slide. . . .

The cold dark water shocked him, pumping even more adrenaline into his system. He clawed at the water, kicking his feet as hard as he could, and swam submerged out the inlet and into open sea.

He gulped air as his head popped up above the surface, expecting to see the cottage up on the rocky promontory. Everything was black! No horizon, no landmarks. He whirled around, disoriented, looking for the shoreline. There! The misty garden lights up on his terrace! He started clawing water, swimming as hard as he could for land.

A minute later he reached a set of wide stone steps carved into the rock that ascended all the way up to his broad terrace.

He pulled his weapon from its holster and raced to the top, taking the steps three at a time.

There he was!

Through an exterior window, he'd caught a glimpse of Spider Payne. He was still out in the hall, slamming his big shoulder against the splintering bedroom door over and over again, screaming loudly in frustration. Hawke sprinted across the terrace, slid open one of the doors, and stepped inside.

The hallway leading to his room was to his immediate left. The house was still pitch-black. He could hear the door begin to give way . . . Spider, illuminated only be the light from within the room, was seconds away from entering.

Moving as quietly as he could, he entered to the darkened hall and paused.

He knew he'd only get one shot at this.

He felt along the wall with his left hand, searching for the overhead hall light switch. Spider was almost completely through the bedroom door . . .

Hawke raised the Colt revolver, sighting on Spider's broad back as he paused to take a breath.

Then he flipped the light switch.

The corridor was instantly flooded with bright incandescent light.

"Spider!" he cried out, the gun now extended with two hands in front of him, standing braced in a shooter's stance.

The big man whirled to face him, his own face a mask of shock and rage. Hawke saw the muzzle of the man's assault rifle come up, Spider already firing rounds, zinging off the tile floor as he raised the automatic weapon toward his enemy hoping to cut him to ribbons.

Hawke fired the Python.

Once into the center of Spider's chest, hoping to catch the seam and his heart.

And once into his right eye.

The man's skull was slammed back against the door. He was still somehow struggling to lift his weapon as he fired blindly . . . rounds still ricocheting off the tile floor as the life drained out of him.

And then and there Spider Payne breathed his last, sliding slowly to the floor, leaving a bloody smear on Alex Hawke's shattered bedroom door, collapsing into a shapeless black heap of useless flesh and bone.

Hawke went to him, knelt down and pressed two fingers to his carotid artery, just to make sure.

No pulse.

The rogue was finally dead.

CHAPTER 15

"Hullo, Ambrose," Hawke said, answering his mobile a few moments later.

"Well, since it appears to be you on the phone, one can only deduce that you survived the encounter."

"Excellent deduction, Constable. One of your best."

"Do you require any assistance, by chance?"

"That would be nice. Where are you? Enjoying a quiet pipe by the fireside somewhere?"

"Hardly. I'm standing about twenty feet outside what used to be your front door, waiting in the pouring rain for all the shooting to die down in there."

"Ah, you're here, then. Well. Do come in, won't you? Doors open, as you can see," Hawke said. "Meet me at the Monkey Bar, will you? We would seem to owe ourselves a libation, some sort of restorative, I suppose. What's your pleasure, old warrior?"

"A gin and bitters should do nicely. Boodles, if you have it."

"I certainly do."

"What about the deceased?"

"Oh, I don't think he'll be having anything this evening. He's moved on."

"Ah. Well, good work, Alex. On my way inside now. I'll see you at the bar."

"Cheerio, then."

"Cheerio."

Hawke looked down at the corpse at his feet. Brass cartridges glittered everywhere on the tile floor. He used one bare foot to roll the man over onto his back, saw one dead black eye staring blindly back at him.

"I should have killed you that night in Tangiers, Payne," he said. "I could have done with one less funeral in Maine, you miserable bastard.".

He found Ambrose standing behind the bar, his cold pipe jammed into one corner of his mouth, pouring a healthy dollop of rum into Hawke's favorite tumbler. Congreve smiled as he poured. "The ambrosial nectar of the gods," he said.

"Indeed."

"What shall we drink to?" Congreve asked, raising his glass of gin.

"Let's see," Hawke mused.

He plucked one of the cigarettes from a silver stirrup cup on the bar, lit up, and thought about it a second before speaking.

"Absent friends and dead enemies?" Hawke said.

And that was the end of it.

Keep reading for an excerpt from
Ted Bell's upcoming novel

WARRIORS

On sale April 2014

PROLOGUE

LORD ALEXANDER HAWKE rose with the dawn.

A shadowy gloom pervaded the gilded coffers of his high-ceilinged bedchamber. He lifted his arms high above his head and stretched mightily, extending his long naked body full length, feeling his muscles and tendons come alive, one by one. Then he wiggled his toes twice for luck and sat straight up beneath the dark blue needlepoint canopy tented above his four bedposts.

His head ached; his lips were dry, and he tried to swallow. Difficult. His mouth felt, perhaps, like that of some ancient Gila monster standing in the middle of the Mojave Desert on a flat rock in the noonday sun. That tequila nightcap, perhaps? Ah, yes, that was it. A dram too far.

Fully awake now, he needed light. There was a discreet control pad on the wall above his bedside table and he reached over to press a pearly button.

A soft whir was followed by the rustle of heavy silk. As the brocade draperies on the many tall French windows drew apart, a soft rosy light began to bloom within the room. Beyond his windows, he saw the red-gold sun perched on the dark rim of the earth. He turned his face toward the sunlight and smiled.

It was going to be another beautiful day.

Beyond his windows lay his walled gardens. Most had been designed by the famous eighteenth-century landscape architect Lancelot Brown. He was a man known to history as "Capability" Brown because the talented and clever Brown slyly told all his potential clients that only their particular estates had the "great capability" to realize his genius.

Beyond the gardens, a tangle of meadows circumscribed by dry stone walls. Then endless forests, temporarily clothed in a light haze of spring green. The narrow lane winding down to the village featured a precarious haystack on a horse-drawn cart, a lone vicar on his wobbly bicycle, and an ancient crone walking stooped beneath a heavy burden. From chimneys of little stone cottages scattered hither and yon, tendrils of grey smoke rose into the pale orange sky.

He had awoken to this chilly morning in early April to watch a grey ground fog swirl up under the eaves and curl around the endless gables and chimneys of the rambling seventeenth-century manor house.

Hawkesmoor, that ancient pile was called. It had

been home to his family for centuries. It was situated amid vast parklands in the gently rolling hills of the Cotswolds, a leisurely two hours' drive north of London on the M40 motorway.

Hawke slid out of bed and into the faded threadbare Levis that lay puddled on the floor where he'd left them at midnight. He pulled an old Royal Navy T-shirt over his head and slipped his bare feet into turquoise-beaded Indian moccasins. They were a particular favorite. He'd bought them during a hunting and fishing expedition with his friends Ambrose Congreve and his fiancée, Lady Diana Mars, to a rustic camp near Flathead Lake, in Montana.

On this particular spring morning, one day before his departure for far more hostile territory, the South China Sea, of all places, Hawke was full of keen anticipation. Four hundred and fifty very powerful horses that even now were stamping their hooves, waiting for him on the apron of bricks in the stable courtyards.

"The Snake," as his new steed was called, was a 1963 Shelby AC Cobra. It was an original, set up for racing by Carroll Shelby himself. With a highly modified 427-cubic-inch engine putting out 450 horsepower, it was capable of achieving speeds nearing 180 miles per hour. It was painted in the famous Cobra racing livery, dark blue with two wide white stripes down the centerline.

It had been purchased by Hawke's man at the Barrett-Jackson auction in Scottsdale, Arizona, and flown to England, arriving by flatbed lorry late the previous afternoon. His primary mechanic, Ian Burns, a fine Irishman with hair and whiskers so blond they were white, gave him a knowing grin. Known forever as "Young Ian," the lad had been going over the Cobra all night, adjusting the timing, checking the plugs, points, and carbs, making sure all was in readiness for Hawke's maiden voyage into the surrounding countryside.

"Quite the brute y've got yerself here now, m'lord," Young Ian said as Hawke approached the car, taking long strides across the mossy brick of the courtyard. "One can see why no one could lay a finger on Dan Gurney and the old 'Snake' at Le Mans back in '64."

"You put a few miles on her this morning, did you, Young Ian?" Hawke asked, smiling and running his hands over the sleek flanks of the beast. "I thought I heard a throaty roar wafting up through the woods earlier."

"Aye, I did indeed."

"And?"

"Still trembling with excitement, m'lord. Can barely handle me socket wrench, sir."

Hawke laughed and gazed at his prize. It was truly a magnificent piece of machinery. A fine addition to his growing but highly selective collection, stored behind the long line of stable doors. A long row that featured, among others, vintage Ferraris, Jags, and Aston-Martins, a black 1956 Thunderbird convertible once owned by Ian Fleming, a spanking-new white McClaren 50, and his cherished daily driver, a steel-grey 1954 Bentley Continental he fondly called "the Locomotive."

"I did, sir. Topped off the petrol tank with avgas, which I highly recommend you use in the car, sir, aviation fuel having much higher octane, obviously. And runs cleaner, sir. The Weber carbs needed a bit of finesse, a couple of belts and hoses needed replacing, but otherwise it's in perfect running order, sir, just as advertised."

"Let's find out, shall we?" Hawke said, grinning from ear to ear.

Hawke climbed behind the wood-rimmed wheel, adjusted the close-fitting racing seat for his six-foot-plus frame, and strapped himself in, using the bright red heavy-duty Simpson racing harness. Then he switched on the ignition.

His glacial blue eyes widened at the instant roar, deafening, really, in the narrow confines of the stone-walled courtyard.

"Bloody hell, Ian!" Hawke grinned, shouting over the thundering engine. "I do believe I feel the stirrings of one falling deeply and passionately in love!"

"As long as y' don' scare the horses, m'lord."

Hawke laughed, a laugh of pure joy.

"Anything at all I should know about?"

"Just one thing, sir. Bit of a steering issue. She seems to want to pull to the right a wee bit. I'll take care of it as soon as you return. Not dangerous, really. I just wanted you to be aware of it in the twisty bits."

"Thanks. Cheerio, then."

Hawke engaged first, mashed the go pedal, popped the clutch, and smoked the squealing tires, fishtailing through the wide wrought-iron stable gates until he reached the paved drive, braked hard, and put the car into a four-wheel drift, a left-hander. He backed off the throttle for the length of the drive, slowing to a stop at the main gate to the estate. The gate was off a two-lane road that led to Chipping Campden, rarely used, and certainly not at this ungodly hour.

Burning rubber once more, he took a hard right out into the road. He had a long straightaway shot in front of him, some miles of clear sailing before the road reentered the forest. There was still a bit of ground fog, but it was blowing around a bit and he had a clear view of the road ahead. He upshifted into second and wound the revs up to redline. He was shoved hard back into his seat, and the scenery became an instant blur.

Ian had been right about the steering.

The Cobra had an annoying habit of pulling to the right. It was irksome but nothing he couldn't handle until he got her back to the stable and corrected it.

HAWKE ENTERED THE dark wood, a place of blue-tinged evergreens.

The macadam road was a twisting snake, but then, he was at the wheel of the Snake. It was narrow, chock-full of inclines, switchbacks, and decreasing radius turns. It was the perfect place to see how his new prize handled. He pushed it hard, not happy unless his tyres were squealing, and the car responded beautifully, enormous torque, precision handling, wedded to splendid racing tyres. Heaven, in other words.

When he finally emerged from the wood, he charged up a rather steep hill, crested it, went fully airborne for a moment, and then sped down into the next straightaway, the engine warmed up now and responding beautifully. He redlined third and upshifted to fourth, then down again to second for the intersection, a tight right-hander into a narrow country lane.

And that's when he heard the blare of air horns behind him.

Christ, he thought, *who the hell?*

He glanced at the rearview mirror and saw the familiar stately grille of an old Rolls-Royce filling the mirror. Right smack on his tail. He slowed, moved left onto the grassy verge, and gestured to the big silver Roller to overtake, for God's sake. He couldn't wait to get a look at the driver. What kind of a moron would even think of trying to pass on this bloody—

A woman. A beautiful woman. Bright yellow Hermès scarf wound round her neck. Silky black hair cut short, and a stunning Asian profile.

She blew the triple air horns again as she blew past, and Hawke's shouted reply surely went unheard over the wind and the combined engine roar. He saw her right arm emerge, hand raised high, ruby red nails, the middle digit extended straight up as she tucked in front of him, almost nicking his front fender.

Fucking hell.

"Balls to the wall, you crazy bitch!" he shouted at her in vain, shaking his righteous fist in disbelieving anger.

And that's when it happened.

He'd taken his right hand off the wheel for a split second, the steering had pulled hard right, and a stout and hardy chestnut tree leaped up out of the woods and smacked him good, pinging both his pride and his new and very shiny blue bonnet in one solid blow.

He forgot the stupid incident over time, but for some reason he never forgot the license plate number on that old silver Roller.

M-A-O.

As in Chairman Mao?

He had no idea. But, as it all turned out in the end, he'd been absolutely spot-on about that damn plate number.

It was Mao.

And the woman behind the wheel? Well, she was indeed one crazy bitch.

CHAPTER 1

BILL CHASE PICKED up the phone and called 1789.

Chase had always thought a year was an odd name for a restaurant. Even for a quaint, colonial eatery in the historic heart of Georgetown. But the year, he knew, was historic: in 1789, George Washington was unanimously elected the nation's first president. In that same year, the United States Constitution went into effect. And also that year, his alma mater, Georgetown University, had been founded.

1789 had been his go-to dining spot in town since his freshman year. The place felt like home, that was all. He loved the elegant high-ceilinged, flower-filled rooms upstairs, usually filled with an eclectic pot-pourri of the well-heeled and the well-oiled, frenetic lobbyists, assorted besotted lovers, gay and straight, illicit and otherwise, various self-delighted junior senators with JFK haircuts, as well as the tired, the careworn, the elderly congressmen.

He liked the restaurant for its authentic colonial vibe, the simple food and subtle service, even the quaint Limoges china. Not to mention the complete absence of pretentious waiters or wine stewards who uttered absurdities like "And what will we be enjoying this evening?"

We? Really? Are you joining us for dinner? Or this little gem he'd heard just last week at Chez Panisse: "And at what temperature would you like your steak this evening, Mr. Chase?" Temperature? Sorry, forgot my meat thermometer this evening. Honestly, who came up with this crap?

1789's utter lack of haute-moderne pretension was precisely what had kept Chase coming back since his college days; those beery, cheery, halcyon days when he'd been a semipermanent habitué of the horseshoe bar at the Tombs downstairs.

Chase hung up the phone in his office, rose from his father's old partner's desk, and stood gazing out the floor-to-ceiling windows. It was late afternoon, and the cold, wintry skies over northern Virginia were laced with streaks of violet and magenta. His private office on the thirtieth floor of Lightstorm's world headquarters had vistas overlooking the Capitol, the White House, and the Pentagon.

To his left he could see Georgetown, Washington's

oldest neighborhood, and home to the Chase family
for generations. The streets of town were already lost
to a grey fog bank. He watched it now, rolling up from
the south and over the silvery Potomac like a misty
tsunami. Traffic on the Francis Scott Key bridge had
become two parallel streams of haloed red and white
lights flowing slowly in opposite directions.

Bill Chase had plenty of reasons to be happy despite the dull grey weather. His marriage had never
been stronger or more passionate, and his new fighter
aircraft prototype, the Lightstorm, had just emerged
victorious in a global battle for a huge Pentagon aeronautical contract. But the best part? His two adored
kids, Milo, age four, and Sarah, age seven, were
healthy, happy, and thriving at school.

Today was a red-letter day. His wife's fortieth.
The Big Four-Oh, as she'd been calling it recently. He
had just booked a table for four upstairs at 1789. His
family would be dining tonight at a cozy round table
in the gracious Garden Room on the second floor,
right next to the fireplace.

BILL CHASE HAD come a long way.

In this decisive year of 2009, he was the fifty-year-
old wunderkind behind Lightstorm Advanced Weapons Systems. LAWS was a global powerhouse whose
rapid rise to the top in the ongoing battle for world
dominance in the military tech industry was the stuff
of legend. Bill himself had acquired a bit of legend.

Fortune magazine's recent cover story on him had been headlined: "One Part Gates, One Part Jobs, One Part Oppenheimer!" His portrait, shot by Annie Leibovitz, showed him smiling in the open cockpit of the new Lightstorm fighter.

The Pentagon had relied heavily on LAWS for the last decade. Chase's firm just been awarded a massive British government contract to develop an unmanned fighter-bomber code-named Sorcerer. It was Bill's pet project: a mammoth bat-wing UAV capable of being launched from Royal Navy aircraft carriers. Heavy payloads, all-weather capability, extreme performance parameters, and zero risk of pilot casualty or death.

An electric crack and a heavy rumble of thunder stirred Chase out of his reverie. He looked up and gazed out his tall windows.

Steep-piled buttresses of thunderheads had towered up darkly. Another mounting bulwark of black clouds to the west, veined with white lightning, was stacking up beyond the Potomac. Big storm coming. He stood at his office window watching the first few fat drops of rain slant across his expansive windows. A stormy night, rain mixed with fog, was on the way and it was too bad.

They had planned to walk the few blocks to the restaurant from their gracious two-hundred-year-old town house just off Reservoir Road.

He wanted the evening to be special in every way. He'd bought Kat a ridiculously expensive piece of jewelry, filled their house with flowers. All day today his wife, Kathleen, had been facing down the Big Four-Oh, and, like most women, she wasn't happy about it.

Kat had been adamant about her big birthday. She'd insisted upon no fancy-pants black-tie party at the Chevy Chase Club, no shindig of any stripe, and, God forbid, not even the merest suggestion of a surprise party.

No. She wanted a quiet dinner out with her husband and their two children. Period.

No cake, no candles.

Bill was feeling celebratory, but he had acquiesced readily. It was, after all, her birthday, not his. Light-years ago, she'd fallen for his southern Bayou Teche drawl and charm; but she'd come to rely on his southern manners. True gents were somewhat in short supply in the nation's capital. And Kat, at least, believed she had found one. Besides his own career, William Lincoln Chase Jr.'s wife and family meant the world to him.

And he tried hard to let them know it, every day of his life.

CHAPTER 2

Georgetown

DINNER WAS LOVELY. The heavy rain had somehow held off, and they'd all walked the five blocks to the restaurant hand in hand, the evening skies a brassy shade of gold, the skeletal trees etched black against them like a Chinese watercolor Chase used to own.

Kat had worn an old black Saint Laurent cocktail dress with slit sleeves that revealed her perfect white arms. She was wearing the diamond brooch at the neckline, the one he'd given her for their twentieth anniversary. The kids, little Milo and his older sister, Sarah, had even behaved, beautifully for them, and for that he was grateful.

Kat didn't like this birthday, with its early hints of mortality, one bit. He was determined to make it a happy evening for her and their family. He'd always had a sense of occasion and he wasn't about to let this one go to waste.

And he'd loved the shine in her lively brown eyes when he gave her the birthday present. She opened the slender black velvet case, took a quick peek, and smiled across the table at him, her eyes sparkling in the candlelight.

A diamond necklace.

"It's lovely, Bill. Really, you shouldn't have. Way too extravagant."

"Do you like it?"

"What girl wouldn't, darling?"

"It's the one Audrey Hepburn wore in *Breakfast at Tiffany's*."

"What?"

"You heard me."

"Bill Chase, stop it. I know when you're teasing."

"No, Kat, really. There was an auction at Sotheby's when I was in New York last week."

"You're serious. Audrey's necklace. The one in the movie."

"Double pinkie swear, crossies don't count."

"Oh. My. God."

"Dad?" Milo said.

"Yes, Milo?"

"You're funny."

Milo and Sarah looked at each other and laughed. Double pinkie swear? They'd never heard their brainy dad speak like that before.

"Audrey Hepburn?" Kat said again, still not quite believing it. "Really?"

"Hmm," he said, "Audrey Hepburn."

It was perfect. For that one fleeting moment, it was all just perfect.

Her favorite actress. Her favorite movie. His favorite girl. The happy smiles on the faces of his two beautiful children.

He was a very, very lucky man, and he knew it.

THE FOG WAS thick when the Chase family stepped outside the flickering gas-lit restaurant entrance. You could barely make out the haloed glow of streetlamps on the far side of the narrow cobblestone Georgetown street.

Bill held his daughter's hand; pausing at the top of the steps, he pulled his grey raincoat closer round his torso. It must have dropped twenty degrees while they were inside, and the fog made everything a little spooky.

They descended the few steps to the sidewalk and turned toward the river.

He could hear that melody in his head, the theme song from his favorite horror movie, *The Exorcist*. What was it called? "Tubular Bells." They'd shot part of that movie on this very same street, on a very foggy night just like this one, and maybe that's why walking back from the Tombs at night sometimes gave him the creeps.

"Let's go, kids, hurry up," Chase said, edgy for some nameless reason as they plunged into the mist.

The street was deserted, for one thing, all the curtains in the town houses drawn tight against the stormy night. He took a look over his shoulder, half expecting to see a deranged zombie dragging one leg behind him.

Nothing, of course.

He felt like an idiot. The last thing he wanted after a perfect evening was to look like a fool and alarm Kat about nothing. She and Sarah were singing "A Foggy Day in London Town" off-key, Kat loving to sing when she'd had a glass or two of her favorite sauvignon blanc.

"Damn it!" Bill cried, bending to grab his knee-cap. Looking over his shoulder, he'd walked right into a fireplug, slammed his knee and upper shin against the hard iron rim. He could feel a warm dampness inside his trouser leg. The cut probably wasn't deep, but it hurt like hell.

"What is it, darling?" Kat said, taking his arm.

"Banged my damn knee, that's all. Let's just keep walking, okay? The corner is just around the corner up there somewhere, I think."

"The corner is just around the corner!" Sarah mimicked and her mother laughed.

What the hell was wrong with him? She was happy. The Big Four-Oh was officially history. And she had loved his present.

"Let's skip. All the way home," he said. "Except

for Dad. For Dad, you see, has a very bum knee." Inexplicably, he felt better. Some second sense had warned him that some bad thing was waiting in the fog.

And it was just a damn fireplug.

CHAPTER 3

IN THE NEXT block he saw a chocolate brown Mercedes-Benz 600 "Pullman" limo pulled over and stopped. It was parked at the curb about twenty feet ahead of them. The 1967 Mercedes Pullman was a classic, the most highly desired limo of the 1960s. He'd been thinking about bidding on one at auction, for Lightstorm's corporate driver.

The interior light was on in the limo, filling the car with soft yellow light. His senses were on high alert, but as he drew near he saw that the occupants were harmless. There was a liveried chauffeur leaning against the rear fender smoking a cigarette; a tiny, elderly couple was seated on the broad leather bench seat in the rear. And there was a diplomatic plate on the big car.

The Chinese delegation.

"Probably that new Chinese ambassador and his

wife," he whispered to Kat. "Looks like they need help."

The passenger door was slightly ajar, and as he drew abreast of them he could see that they were plainly lost in the fogbound streets of old Georgetown. The wife, snow white hair held back in a chignon, wearing a mink stole over a black cashmere turtleneck with a strand of pearls, had a well-creased road map of D.C. spread across her lap.

Her husband was peering over her shoulder, pointing his finger at an intersection and asking the chauffeur something about the Estonian embassy.

"May I help you?" Chase asked in English, never trusting his always rusty Mandarin. He bent down to speak to the ambassador's wife.

She looked up in surprise; apparently she hadn't seen his approach in the fog.

"Oh," the elegant woman said sweetly in English, "aren't you kind, dear? We're embarrassed to say it, but we're late for a reception and completely lost. My husband, the ambassador, and I are new to Washington, you see, and haven't yet got a clue, as you Americans say. We're looking for the Estonian embassy . . . even our poor driver cannot find it."

Chase leaned down to get a closer look at her map.

"Well," he said, reaching inside to point out their location on the map. "Here you are. And here's Wisconsin Street over here and the embassy is right—"

The woman clamped her small but incredibly powerful hand around his wrist. In an instant, she had pulled him forward, off his feet, halfway into the car.

The husband had something in his hand, a hypo, and he plunged it into the side of Chase's neck. He could feel a wave of nausea instantly sweep over him, tried to pull away but had no muscle power at all.

"Try to relax, Dr. Chase," the woman cooed softly. "It will all be over in a second or two."

She knew his name.

"Kat, grab Milo! Sarah! Run! Run!" Bill Chase cried over his shoulder. Kat looked at him for a second in astonishment, saw he was serious, and gathered Milo and Sarah up into her arms. And started running. He saw them run, then lost them, folding into the swirling fog.

It was the last time, he truly believed at that moment, that he would ever see them alive.

He was vaguely aware of a white van passing the limo, headed in the direction of his family. Next he was being manhandled by the chauffeur around to the rear of the Mercedes. The big man popped the massive trunk, lifted him easily, and dropped him inside.

The lid of the trunk slammed down.

All was blackness then.

KAT, WHO WAS losing her mind to terror, tried to run. But the fog, two children in her arms, and her damn Jimmy Choo heels made it all but impossible. All she wanted to do was speed-dial 911 on her cell, get the police, and—

A van swerved up to the curb just beside her. The

rear doors flew open, and four large men all in black leaped to the pavement right in front of them. They were wearing ski masks, Kat saw, as one of them, his body enwreathed with fog, stepped under the hazy streetlamp to snatch Milo from her arms.

She cried out, ripping Milo away again, clutching her son's frail little body to her chest, and that's when something unbelievably hard, a ball of pain encased in steel, struck the back of her head. It made a dull, sickening noise and sent her sprawling to the ground, her pulse roaring in her ears, her face half submerged in a large puddle with fat raindrops dancing upon it.

She knew she was close to blacking out.

"Milo!" she cried out, raising her head to search for her children. "Sarah!"

But they had disappeared into the turning wisps and wraiths of fog that hovered around the white van. And one of the four thugs had taken them from her. The one who had hit her now had her by the ankles, dragging her toward the van, her head bouncing over the cobblestones.

Just before she slipped into blackness she saw one of the men pulling her limp son up into the rear of the van. The man who was yanking Milo and Sarah inside by the arm, his face hidden by the black balaclava, was screaming at her son. Unintelligible threats in some guttural foreign language . . . Chinese, perhaps.

What in God's name was going on?

CHAPTER 4

South China Sea
Present Day

MIDNIGHT. NO MOON, no stars, the sea a flat black void a few feet beneath his wingtips. For a man streaking through the night over hostile waters approaching the speed of sound, at an altitude no sane man would even dare consider, Commander Alex Hawke was remarkably comfortable. He was piloting an F-35C Lightning. The new matte-black American-built fighter jet was one of many purchased and heavily modified by Britain's Royal Navy for under-the-radar special ops just like this one.

Lord Alexander Hawke, a former Royal Navy fighter pilot and decorated combat veteran of the latest Gulf War, now a seasoned British intelligence officer with MI6, had to smile.

The F-35C's single seat reclined at an angle of exactly thirty degrees, transforming the deadly Lightning, Hawke thought, into something along the lines of a chaise longue. Leave it to the bloody Americans to worry about fighter pilot "comfort" during a dogfight. Still, it was comfy enough, he had to admit, smiling to himself. Rather like a supersonic Barcalounger!

His eyes flicked over the dimly lit instrument array and found nothing remotely exciting going on. Even the hazy reddish glow inside the cockpit somehow reassured him. He was less than six hundred nautical miles from his designated speck on the map, the tiny island of Xiachuan, and closing fast.

Every mile he put behind him lessened the chance of a Chinese Suchoi 33 jet interceptor or a surface-to-air missile blasting him out of the sky. Although the Lightning was equipped with the very latest anti-missile defense systems, the Lightning was no stealth fighter.

He was vulnerable and he knew it.

Should he be forced to eject and be captured by the Red Chinese, he'd be tortured mercilessly before he was executed. A British intelligence officer flying an unmarked American fighter jet had no business entering Chinese airspace. But he did have business in China, very serious business, and his success might well help avert impending hostilities that could lead to regional war. At that point the chances of it expanding into a global conflict were nearly one hundred percent.

Preventing that was his mission.

IN LONDON, ONE week earlier, "C," as the chief of MI6 was traditionally called, had summoned Hawke to join him for lunch at his men's club, Boodle's. Lord Hawke had thought it was a purely social invitation. Usually the old man conducted serious SIS business only within the sanctum sanctorum of his private offices at 85 Albert Embankment, the headquarters for Six.

So it was that a very relaxed Alex Hawke presented himself promptly at the appointed hour of noon.

"Well, here you are at last," C said, amiably enough. The "at last" was the old boy's way of letting you know who was boss. Sir David Trulove, a gruff old party thirty years Hawke's senior, had his customary corner table at the third-floor Grill Room. Shafts of dusty sunlight pouring down from the tall leaded windows set the table crystal and silver afire, all sparkle and gleam. Above C's table, ragged tendrils of his tobacco smoke hung in wreaths and coils, turning and twisting slowly in the sunlit space.

The dining and drinking at Boodle's was, by any standard, done in one of the poshest man caves in all London.

C took a spartan sip of his gin and bitters, looked his young subordinate up and down in cursory fashion, and said, "I must say, Alex, a bit of time in the down mode becomes you. You're looking rather fit and ready for the fray. 'Steel true, blade straight,' as Conan Doyle's memorable epitaph would have it. Sit, sit."

Hawke sat. He paid scant attention to C's flattery,

knowing the old man used it sparingly and only to his own advantage, usually as some prelude to another more important subject. Whatever was on his mind, he seemed jovial enough.

"Most kind of you, sir. I've been looking forward to this luncheon all week. I get bored silly sometimes, up in the country. Good being back in town. This is a much-needed interlude, I must say."

"Let's see if you still feel that way at the conclusion. What are you drinking? My club, my treat, of course," Trulove said, catching a roving waiter's eye.

"Gosling's, please. The Black Seal, neat."

Hawke sat back and smiled. It really was good to be here, a place where a man could act like a man wants to act, and do just what he pleased without encountering approbation from bloody anybody.

"So," Hawke said after C had ordered another drink and his rum, "trouble, I take it."

"No end of it, sadly."

"Spill the beans, sir. I can take it."

"The bloody Chinese again."

"Ah, my dear friends in the Forbidden City. Something new? I thought I was fairly well up to speed."

"Well, Alex, you know those inscrutable Mandarins in Beijing as well as I do. Always some new wrinkle up their embroidered red silk sleeves. It's that abominable situation in the South China Sea, I'm afraid."

"Heating up?"

"Boiling over."

Hawke's rum arrived. He took a sip of it and said, "What now, sir? Don't tell me the Reds have blockaded one of the world's busiest trade routes?"

"No, no, not yet anyway. It may come to that. Still, simply outrageous behavior. First, they unilaterally extend their territorial claims in the South China Sea hundreds of miles south and east from their most southerly province of Hainan. All done with zero regard for international maritime law, of course. And now they have established a no-fly zone over a huge U-shaped sea area that overlaps parts of Vietnam, the Malay Peninsula, the Philippines, Taiwan, and Brunei."

"Good Lord. And with what possible justification?"

"Beijing says its right to the area comes from two thousand years of history, when the Paracel and Spratly island chains were regarded as integral parts of the Chinese nation. Vietnam says, rightly, that both island chains lie entirely within its territory. That it has actively ruled over both chains since the seventeenth century and has the documents to prove it."

A flash of anger flared in Hawke's eyes.

"Bastards have created a flashpoint as dangerous as the Iranians and the Strait of Hormuz, haven't they? Clearly global conflict implications."

"Spot-on. And now they've begun insisting that every aircraft transiting these formerly wide-open routes must first ask permission of the Chinese government. Including U.S. and Royal Navy flights. Outrageous. We will not, bloody hell, ask them permission for any such thing! Nor will anyone else, I can guarantee you that."

"The result?"

"It's all a ruse to provoke a reaction. The new-generation Chinese warrior is a fervent nationalist, with militaristic veins bulging with pride. And, the Chinese are, as we speak, using their North Korean stooges to probe and prod at our will to prevail in this region, both at sea and in the air. I mean, you've got NK coastal patrols 'bumping' into the Yank's Seventh Fleet in the night, near collisions with Royal Navy vessels, that sort of thing, spoiling for a fight. The North Koreans, of course, know China will back them up in a showdown."

"An extremely dangerous game."

"To say the very least."

"And the Western countermove?"

"It gets tricky. Under President Tom McCloskey's strong leadership, the United States is taking a very hard line with China. The U.S. Navy is dramatically increasing its naval presence in the region, of course. The Seventh Fleet is en route to the Straits of Taiwan. And they've deployed U.S. Marines to Darwin, on the western coast of Australia. Meanwhile, our own PM, in a weak moment, actually had an extraordinary idea."

"He did?"

"I know, I know, no one believes it was actually his original notion, but that's the official story coming out of Number Ten Downing."

"What's his extraordinary thought?"

"He suggests the allies consider a massive convoy, Alex. Warships from the Royal Navy, Japan, Taiwan, the Philippines, Vietnam, and the Yanks with an entire carrier battle group, the USS *Theodore Roosevelt,* along with seven or eight other countries. Full steam ahead right up their bloody arses and we'll see what they bloody do about it, won't we?"

C laughed and drained his drink.

"Well, for starters," Hawke said, "the Chinese may elect to take out a massive U.S. carrier with one of their new advanced killer satellites the CIA was describing to our deputy directors and section heads just last week. It's not beyond the realm of plausibility."

"Hmm, the life of a country squire has not completely numbed your frontal lobe capacity. But you're right. That is a consideration, Alex. At any rate, right now, the prime minister's notion is only a good idea. Hardly a done deal, as they say."

"Why?"

"Simple. A few pantywaists in the U.S. Congress are thus far unwilling to go along with the PM's scheme for fear of losing one of their big billion-dollar float babies. So, alas, our convoy scheme is paralyzed at the moment. But, look, we're not going to sit around on our arses and let this stand. No, not for one blasted moment!"

"What are we going to do about it, sir?"

"You mean, what are you going to do about it, dear boy. That's why I'm springing for lunch."

"Ah, yes, of course. No free lunch, as they say."

"Damn right. Never has been. Not in this man's navy, at any rate."

"How can I help, sir? I've been sitting on the sidelines for far too long. I've got grass and flowers growing up through the soles of my shoes."

C looked around to establish whether anyone was within earshot. The aural perimeter thus secured, he said, "We at Six have established a back-channel communication with a high-ranking Chinese naval officer. Three-star admiral, in fact. Someone with a working brain in his head. Someone who does not want go to war over his own government's deliberate and insane maritime provocations any more than we do."

Hawke leaned forward. The hook, having been set, now drew him nigh to the old master.

"This sounds good."

"It is. Very."

"Congratulations, sir."

"What makes you think this one is mine, Alex?"

"A wild guess."

"Well. Nevertheless."

"So," Hawke said, "the Chinese are well aware that they cannot possibly afford to go to war with the West now. In a decade? Perhaps. But not now. They haven't got the bottle for it. And, moreover, they haven't got the arsenal."

"Of course not. According to our chaps on both sides of the pond, they are at least five to ten years behind the West in terms of advanced weaponry. And I mean both in the air and on the sea. No, it's an obvious political ploy, albeit an extremely dangerous one."

"To what end?"

"Simple. They wish to divert attention away from their burgeoning internal domestic turmoil, particularly Tibet, and the daily insanity run rampant in their 'client state,' North Korea. Thus this bellicose show of force. Show the peasant population and the increasingly restive middle class just how big, bad, and powerful the new boys are."

"Sheer insanity."

"Our world and welcome to it. But you, and I do mean you, Alex Hawke, with a little help from me, are going to put a stop to it. Even if it's only a stopgap, temporary measure. I intend to buy us some time for diplomacy or other stratagems."

"Tell me how, sir."

"Operation Pacifist. Clever, eh? You'll be reporting solely to me on this. Any information is strictly need-to-know. I have arranged a secret rendezvous for you. You will be meeting with a high-ranking Chinese admiral, whose name is Tsang, on a small island in a remote quadrant of the South China Sea. An uninhabited bit of paradise known as Xiachuan Island. Tsang wants to talk about a way he sees out of this extraordinarily dangerous confrontation with the West. Then it will become a matter of whether or not we can get the PM and Washington to go along with whatever proposals you come home with."

"Why me?"

"Security. He said any meeting with our side had to be conducted in absolute secrecy, for obvious reasons, and that he wanted a completely untraceable contact. In a remote location known only to him and me. Together we selected Xiachuan Island. Completely deserted for years. It was home to a World War II Japanese air force base, but abandoned because of Japan's current territorial dispute with China."

"How does one visit this island paradise?"

"One flies. There is a serviceable eight-thousand-foot airstrip there that should accommodate you nicely."

"What kind of bus shall I be driving?"

"An American F-35C Lightning. One of ours. Especially modified for nighttime insertions. All the latest offensive and defensive goodies, I assure you. Kinetic energy weapons and all that. The sort of thing you enjoy."

"Lovely airplane. Always wanted another crack at one."

"Well, my boy, you'll get one. First thing tomorrow morning, in fact. I've already cleared your calendar. You'll report at seven to Lakenheath RAF. Three days of intensive flight training in the Lightning with a USAF chief instructor off your wingtip. Courtesy of CIA and President McCloskey's White House. Then off you go into the wild blue yonder."

"Aye-aye, sir. I think McCloskey has shown rather a lot of courage in this Chinese showdown. He's a hard-liner and just what we need at present. I just hope he keeps his wits about him. These are dangerous waters we're entering, full of political mines and razor-sharp shoals."

"Indeed. The mainstream American press is hounding the president relentlessly, aren't they? Look at his poll numbers. He just needs to stand his ground against this senseless Chinese and North Korean bullying."

"Hmm. One thing if I may. This admiral, how high ranking is he, exactly? I mean to say, is he powerful enough to actually defuse this latest crisis?"

"High enough. He is the Chinese chief of naval operations."

Hawke smiled. "Start at the top and work your way up. Isn't that what you've always told me?"

"Indeed."

"And how much of a gratuity am I going to be transporting to the good admiral in return for all this assistance in defusing the global crisis from the inside?"

"One hundred million pounds sterling. Cash. In a lockbox you'll carry in the cockpit with you."

Hawke whistled and said, "That's all?"

"If you succeed, it's worth every shilling. Now, let's order some lunch and talk of more pleasant things. I understand our mutual friend, Ambrose Congreve, is to be wed next Christmas. I assume you're to be best man?"

"Well . . . to be honest, I don't really know. I would assume so. But I haven't heard from him on the subject."

"Didn't mean to step into that one."

"Not at all. Perhaps they've called the whole thing off and he simply hasn't the heart to tell me."

Sir David picked up his menu and began to study it intently.

"Well. You will find an obsessively complete dossier on Operation Pacifist waiting for you when you get home to Hawkesmoor. Motorcycle courier just dropping it off with Pelham now. Memorize it and burn it. Now, then, Alex, what will you be having for lunch?"

"Not sure, sir. What looks expensive?"

CHAPTER 5

The White House

PRESIDENT TOM MCCLOSKEY stared at the live feed from the East China Sea. He was, he knew in some secret part of him, in a state of shock. Hell, all of them were in shock—McCloskey himself; his close friend since Annapolis, Vice President David Rosow; his beautiful new and wildly popular secretary of state, Kim Oakley Case; the always reliable secretary of defense, Anson Beard; and the chairman of the Joint Chiefs, Charlie Moore.

And all the rest of the crisis team; every one of them had been staring at the Situation Room screens for over an hour.

What they were seeing up there was real-time terror. Innocent American lives were being threatened half a world away, and there was not one damn thing he or anybody else in the White House or over at State, CIA, or the Pentagon could do about it. Not one damn thing.

"Shit," he whispered under his breath. "Shit."

China and her increasingly bellicose surrogate, North Korea, as of forty-eight hours ago, were staging joint naval war games in the East China Sea. North Korea had made a big show of it for the press, trotting out their latest warships. According to his most recent CIA naval intelligence briefing, and some help from British intelligence, it was clear that China had long been planning to use the North Korean navy as a pawn in this little game of their own. Test American resolve.

But how?

Nobody at CIA, State, the Pentagon, or any other intelligence agency had prepared him for this. This was a goddamn nightmare, and it couldn't have come at a worse time. The whole country was coming unglued over a few inadvertent remarks he'd made at the G7 summit in Prague the week before. Jesus Christ. The media, no friends of his in the run-up to the damn election, were all over him for a couple of misstatements he'd made to Putin about China.

The joint press event was over and done with and he'd assumed the mikes were dead. Reasonable assumption.

They weren't.

What he'd said was innocent enough. The once-powerful Putin, now increasingly in danger of becoming China's bitch, was playing hardball with the United States over China's currency manipulations. And McCloskey hadn't come this far to be backed into a corner by the Russian's trumped-up tough-guy act, and he was planning to draw a line in the sand and call the Russian's bluff. But he wasn't going to tell Putin that, no sir. He was going to sow a few seeds of disinformation and let the Kremlin show its cards. His own wife had told him what a shrewd idea it was, f'crissakes.

So what he said to the Russian was, "Prime Minister, just give me a little wiggle room here. Just enough to get through the All-Asia Conference next month. After that, I can show a lot more flexibility. Trust me."

And for that, a few offhand comments taken completely out of context, he was paying a steep price. Using up a lot of political capital to hold his fragile coalition together. Had the Senate whip and the Speaker of the House breathing down his neck, wanting him to issue a clarifying statement.

Hell, he had Tom Friedman and the *New York Times* questioning his fitness for office. The *Washington Post*! The *Post* ran a goddamn editorial in the most recent Sunday edition headlined "Is He Losing It?" Well, so be it. Politics at this level was a game for those who could take the heat, stay in the kitchen, and keep their heads in the fucking oven.

And now this!

At 0441 hours GMT, a North Korean fast-attack

warship had deliberately rammed and disabled a small and lightly armed U.S. Navy surveillance vessel now taking on water in the disputed international region of the East China Sea. It was a moonless night, there was fog, but there was no conceivable excuse for the USN captain's behavior.

In a state of relatively minor duress, he had folded his cards and surrendered his vessel to the North Koreans, for God's sake. Was the U.S. skipper insane?

The U.S. boat was CIA, of course, but the captain of the North Korean vessel didn't know that. All he knew was that his claim of territorial incursion and his demand to board (backed up by overwhelming firepower) had been granted by the U.S. skipper.

Now, the president of the United States and his team watched as four young able-bodied American seamen, bound and blindfolded, were kneeling side by side with their backs against a steel bulkhead on the foredeck of their vessel.

The American skipper and his crew were being held at gunpoint up on the bridge. God knew what was going up there, McCloskey thought, feeling a sense of impotent rage come close to overwhelming him.

An oddly tall and lean Korean officer was screaming at the four captives, bending down, getting right up into their faces.

"What's that bastard saying?" McCloskey said to the State Department translator.

He told him.

"Son of a bitch," the president muttered.

"He's got a gun!" someone at the table said.

The NK navy officer stepped in front of one of the Americans and stuck a large black automatic pistol up under his chin. The officer was red-faced and screaming at the sailor now, venting all his pent-up hatred and anger on the helpless sailor.

Everyone in the room saw the blindfolded youth working his mouth and knew instantly what would happen next.

"Don't do it, boy!" General Charles Moore, chairman of the Joint Chiefs said to the screen. "Don't give that bastard any excuse, son! None, no way, never."

"Oh, Christ," McCloskey said, "no, no, no."

The sailor spat, catching the hysterical officer square in the face.

The Korean officer recoiled in anger, using the sleeve of his uniform to wipe away the saliva.

He suddenly raised his arm and drove the pistol into the sailor's face, smashing his nose into a red pulp.

"Sonofabitch!" the president said, leaning forward, his face twisted in anger.

Further enraged by the sight of blood, the North Korean officer put the barrel of his automatic between the young American's eyes . . . and pulled the trigger.

The dead sailor slumped forward, facedown on the cold wet deck.

"Tell me I'm not seeing this," the president said, unable to tear his eyes away from the screen.

"He's going to execute all four," General Moore said in a steady voice that sounded oddly detached.

And, as they all watched in abject horror, that is exactly what he did. Head shots, at close range.

A pin could drop.

"Turn that damn thing off," the president said.

"Off, Mr. President?"

"Isn't that what I just said?"

An ashen-faced aide made a throat-cutting motion, and the monitors all went black at once.

"That's better, isn't it?" McCloskey said, propping his polished cowboy boots on an empty chair and firing up a Marlboro.

No one said a word.

"It's a bitch, ain't it?" the president said to no one in particular. "Four of our boys dead. The goddam NKs in possession of one of our CIA shit-buckets chock-full of classified information. Damn it to hell. Somebody give me a good reason not to turn North Korea into a goddamn NK-Mart parking lot. China, too, if they dick around with our navy anymore. I'm serious. I'll tell you all one thing. I'd like to know what Admiral Wainwright has to say about all this. Tony? What the hell am I going to do now?"

A palpable pall of shocked silence hung over the room.

"Tony?" the president repeated, swiveling around, searching all the faces in the room.

Finally, someone had the guts to speak up. Secretary of State Kim Case, which surprised no one.

"Mr. President?" the slim, attractive blonde said.

"Yeah, Kim, what is it?"

"Admiral Wainwright is dead, sir. He died in the terrorist attack on the *Dreadnought* in Tripoli last May."

The president was very quiet for a long time before he looked up, staring at the secretary, his face a stone mask.

"I know that, Kim. What I said was, I'd like to know what he thought. And I would like to know that, I really would. But he's dead. Isn't he?"

"Yes, Mr. President. He is."

A stunned silence descended.

No one said a word. What more was there to say?

Emily Young, the president's lovely young personal secretary, could be heard sobbing quietly in dark corner of the room. Emily didn't think she could take much more of this. She loved the old cowboy. Actually was in love with him. It killed her to see the boss like this, a wounded stag. And all of them, the press, with their goddamn knives out . . . and, like a mule in a hailstorm, he just had to stand there and take it.

She heard the president say, "Emily, for crissakes, will you stop bawling? What the hell is wrong with everybody?"

There was no answer.

The president stood, looked around at all the upturned faces, and said, "Well, thank you everyone. We'll reconvene in one hour."

After they filed out, he sat back down again, gazing absently into the middle distance, smoking his Marlboro down to a bright orange coal. He'd never felt so lost and alone in his life.

THE WHITE HOUSE sous-chef looked beat.

It was almost midnight on a Friday night and, for Chef Tommy Chow, it had already been a very long week. First thing Monday morning, Matt Lauer and the whole damn *Today* show crew had shown up early for a live broadcast and wanted breakfast. Then the lavish state dinner for the prime minister of England, the Rose Garden luncheon the First Lady held annually for the Daughters of the American Revolution, and on and on, no rest for the weary.

And now he'd gotten a last-minute call from the ranking West Wing staffer saying the president had invited a few of his closest cabinet members for an impromptu breakfast in the morning. Talk about China and North Korea, Tommy imagined. Hell, that's all they ever talked about lately.

"Go home, Tommy," one of his guys said. "You look exhausted. We can finish the prep by ourselves."

"No. I insist. You guys head out. I promised the boss man I'd take care of this breakfast thing and I'm going to do it. Seriously, get the hell out of here and go home to your families, okay? I got no family. Not here in Washington anyway. Leave the graveyard shift to me. Okay?"

"You got it, boss. Have it your way," the pastry chef said, and they all bolted for the exits.

Chow waited until the last one had left before he began prepping tomorrow's cabinet breakfast. Huevos rancheros, the presidential favorite, home fries, frijoles refritos with melted Monterey Jack, rashers of bacon and jalapeño-flavored sausage patties, honey biscuits, and hot sauce. Tex-Mex, they called it. Hardly his idea of haute cuisine, but they didn't care for that much upstairs anymore.

A rueful smile flitted across Chow's face as he stirred what he privately referred to as his "secret sauce" into the president's eggs.

The graveyard shift, he mouthed silently.

Truer words would never be spoken.

Not in this White House, anyway.

CHAPTER 6

South China Sea

A LOUD, KEENING wail suddenly filled the Lightning's cockpit. Holy mother of God, Hawke thought, he'd just been painted by enemy radar!

He whipped his head around and saw the Chinese SAM missile's fiery flame signature streaking up toward his Lightning, dead on his six, homing in on the afterburner. By the speed of the incoming, he guessed it to be one of the newer Hong Qi 61s. Where the hell had it come from? Some kind of new Chinese radar-proof shore battery on a nearby atoll? None of his so-called sophisticated gadgetry had even picked the damn thing up!

He hauled back on the stick and instantly initiated a vertical climb, standing the Lightning on its tail and rocketing skyward like something launched

from Canaveral in the good old days. He deployed
chaff aft and switched on all the jamming devices located in the airplane's tail section. He was almost instantly at forty thousand feet and climbing, his eyes
locked on the missile track displayed on his radar and
thermal imaging screens. Its unverified speed, Hawke
knew, was Mach 3.

It was closing fast.

The deadly little bastard blew right through his
chaff field without a single degree of deviation. The
Chinese weapon was not behaving in accordance
with MI6 and CIA assessments of their military capability. With every passing second, his appointment
with imminent death went from possible to probable.
He'd have to depend on the Lightning's jamming devices and his own evasive maneuvers if he was going
to survive this attack.

He nosed the F-35C over and put it into a screaming vertical dive. He was now gaining precious seconds. The Hong Qi would now have to recalculate
the target, alter course, and get on his six again. He'd
known from the instant the SAM missile appeared
on his screen that there was only one maneuver that
stood any chance at all of saving him.

A crash dive.

Straight down into the sea.

Hairy, but sometimes effective, Hawke knew
from long experience. To succeed, he had to allow
the deadly missile to get extraordinarily close to
impacting and destroying his aircraft. So close that

when he pulled out of the dive at the last possible instant, the nose of his airplane would be so near the water's surface that the missile would have zero time to correct before it hit the water at Mach 3, vaporizing on impact.

"You've got to dip your nose in the water, son," an old flight instructor had told him once about the maneuver. "That's the only way."

The missile had now nosed over in a perfect simulation of Hawke's maneuver and homed in on the diving jet. He watched it closing at a ridiculous rate of speed.

His instruments and screeching alarms were all telling him he was clearly out of his bloody mind. The deeply ingrained human instinct to run, to change course and evade, clawed around the edges of his conscious mind. But Hawke had the warrior's ability to erect a firewall around it, one that was impenetrable in times like this.

It was those few precious white-hot moments precisely like this one that Alex Hawke lived for. At his squalling birth, his father had declared him "a boy born with a heart for any fate." And, like his father and grandfather before him, he was all warrior, right down to the quick, and he was bloody good at it. His focus at this critical moment, fueled by adrenaline, was borderline supernatural . . . his altimeter display screen was a jarring blur, but he didn't see it; the collision-avoidance alarms were howling in his headphones, but he didn't hear them. His grip on the stick was feather light, his breathing calm and measured, his hands bone dry and surgeon steady.

His mind was now quietly calculating the differential between the seconds remaining until the missile impacted the Lightning and the seconds until the aircraft impacted the sea. Ignoring everything, the wail of the screeching sirens and the flashing electronic warnings, the pilot began his final mental countdown.

The surface of the sea raced up at him at a dizzying rate . . .

Five . . . four . . . three . . . two . . .

NOW!

He hauled back on the stick.

The nose literally splashed coming up, and he saw beads of seawater racing across the exterior of his canopy. He'd caught the crest of a wave pulling out of the dive . . . He felt the G forces building . . .

You got to dip your nose in the water, son.

Made it.

He barely registered the impact of the missile hitting the water over the roar of his afterburners. But he heard it, all right. He was in the clear and initiating a climb out as he visualized it: the SAM vaporizing upon contact with the concrete hard surface of the sea at such speed . . .

The G forces were fierce. He began his quick climb back to his former below-the-radar altitude.

And that's when his starboard wingtip caught a huge cresting wave that sent his aircraft spinning out of control. Where the hell had that come from . . . He was suddenly skimming over the sea like a winged Frisbee. He felt a series of severe jolts as the fuselage made contact, and he instinctively understood that the aircraft was seconds away from disintegrating right out from under his doomed arse . . .

He reached down to his right and grabbed the red handle, yanked it, and the canopy exploded upward into the airstream and disappeared. The set of rocket motors beneath his seat instantly propelled him up and out of the spinning cockpit and straight into the black night sky.

Seconds later, his primary chute deployed and he had a bird's-eye view of his airplane as it metamorphosed into varying sizes and shapes of scrap metal and disappeared beneath the waves.

Along with the five hundred million in the lockbox, he thought. Not only had his mission just gone straight to hell, it was a very bloody expensive failure.

He yanked the cord that disengaged him from his seat and watched it fall away as he floated down. Moments later his boots hit the water. It was cold as hell, but he started shedding gear as quickly as he could. He was unhurt, or it seemed that way, and he started treading water while his life jacket inflated. *So far, so good,* he thought, managing to keep his spirits aloft surprisingly well for a downed airman all alone in this dark world.

Normally, there'd be an EPIRB attached to his shoulder harness. Upon contact with the water, it would immediately begin broadcasting his GPS co-ordinates to a passing friendly satellite. Normally, he could just hang out for a while here in the South China Sea and wait for one of Her Majesty's Navy rescue choppers to come pluck him from the soup and winch him aboard. Normally. But, of course, this was a secret transit and he had no distress radio beacon, no EPIRB. He had exactly nothing.

He knew the water temperature was cold enough to kill him eventually. The thermal body suit he wore would stave off hypothermia long enough for him to have a slim shot at survival.

He spun his suspended body through 360 de-grees. Nothing of note popped out of the darkness. No lights on the horizon, no silver planes in the sky. Nada, zip, zero. Nothing but the vastness of black stretching away in all directions . . . no EPIRB equals NO hope of immediate rescue. He was some fifty miles off the southern coast of mainland China.

If he was lucky, and he usually was, he was in a shipping channel. If not, sayonara. He looked at his dive watch, whistling a chirrupy tune about sunshine and lollypops. Five hours minimum to sunrise.

He began to whistle a song his father had taught him for use at times like this.

Nothing to do but hang here in frozen limbo and wait to see what happens next.

And maybe pray a little.

CHAPTER 7

The White House

"IT'S THE PRESIDENT," the First Lady said, gripping the phone so tightly her knuckles shone bone white through her pink skin. "I can't seem to wake him up."

"Is he breathing?"

"Yes, I-I think so. His chest is moving."

"Don't worry. We're on our way up now. The whole team. Stay calm," Ken Beer, the White House physician said, and the line went dead.

"TOM," SHE SAID, shaking him by the shoulders. "Tom, wake up, damn it!"

Nothing.

Had he taken something? She scoured the bedroom and medicine cabinet for empty vials. Nothing. She'd seen him depressed before, but the mood swings were getting terrifying lately. Still, suicide? No. Out of the question. He would never do that. Too narcissistic. Far too invested in his place in history and his date with destiny, the showdown with China coming up in Hong Kong next month.

It had been two days since the disastrous meeting in the Situation Room. The entire household was abuzz with rumors about what had really happened in there. Her assistants and household spies were reporting back to her with everything they were picking up. He was drunk. He was stoned on meds. He was losing his marbles. He wasn't fit to be president. *60 Minutes* was doing a segment called "The Incredible Vanishing President." He was sick. It was dangerous. He had early-onset Alzheimer's just like Ronnie Reagan. They had to rally round him. They had to protect him . . .

Blah-blah-blah.

And then her reverie was broken as the private quarters was suddenly full of people. Secret Service, medical techs with defibrillators, portable EKGs, and God knows what all. Ken Beer was running the show, which was good; she'd had total confidence in him since that incident aboard *Air Force One* the year before.

She tried to read something into Ken's expression, but he had his game face on. All business. He had taken her aside after his initial examination and asked her if she wanted a lorazepam. She'd refused, but wondered if maybe she needed one. He looked so . . . gone . . . lying there, all the IV tubes and EKG wires taped to his chest and—

"Okay," Ken said, taking her by the arm and walking her quickly into the sitting room where they could speak privately. "Here's the deal. His vitals are good. Strong. But he's in a coma. I don't think it's a stroke. No coronary issues. I'm having blood work done right now, but I don't want to wait for it. You with me?"

"Keep talking."

"Right. He's going to Walter Reed right now. Okay? That's the best thing for him. The safest, most conservative option. I've already called it in."

"Is he going to come out of it? The coma?"

"Qualified answer? Yes. He's going to come out of it. Listen. Don't you worry. We'll take good care of him. Do you want to ride in the ambulance with him?"

"Of course I do, Ken. Do you even have to ask me that?"

"Sorry. My mistake. The president's already on his way down to the South Portico. Let's go."

TOMMY CHOW MET his U.S. handler at the Capitol Grill for drinks the afternoon the president was admitted to Walter Reed Hospital. The Grill was a mecca for secretaries, staffers, lobbyists, and bureaucrats of every stripe and strata in D.C. Tommy knew one of the Chinese waiters, a guy who always made sure they got a quiet table in the back. Even if they were noticed, and it was very unlikely, a low-level staffer from State and a noncelebrity chef from 1600 having a martini or three wouldn't cause anyone's radar to light up.

"Is he dead yet, T?"

George, his State Department friend, whispered to him after they'd finished one drink. George (he never used his last name) was tall and thin, with brown hair parted neatly down the middle. He had thick black eyebrows over a large straight nose, thin lips, and a receding chin. He was always nattily dressed in a three-piece Brooks Brothers suit, preppy striped bow tie. Somebody named Tucker Carlson was his fashion muse, he'd once told Tommy Chow. Tucker who?

George, ex-military, and a semi big shot at State, had one of those thin fake smiles that made you hate him instantly. He had a degree in aeronautics from Stanford and a law degree from Yale. He was also one of those guys who truly believed he was always the smartest guy in the room.

The kind of guy who usually got caught. Which was fine with Tommy, as long as he didn't take Tommy Chow down with him.

"CNN is now saying he's still fading in the ICU. Matter of hours. True? Or false?" George said with a fake quizzical expression.

"No. You know damn well he's not dying."

"So. False information. Bad, Wolf Blitzer, bad, bad, bad. Snow White's poisoned jalapeño pie didn't do the trick, huh, little Tommy? C'mon. Let's take a little stroll around the nation's capital."

"It's raining, George."

"Yeah. It does that. Man up, little buddy. You need to get out more."

Chow paid the check as always and they left the noisy Grill, now filling up with good-looking girls who'd all come to Washington from the provinces, looking for a job but down on their knees praying every night for a lobbyist or even a senator or two.

Chow was silent for the first few blocks. Now they had sought shelter under the trees near the reflecting pool. No one around.

Chow was saying, "Shit. I just don't know what happened. After the navy taster had approved the president's tray, I stirred enough bad mushroom puree into that meat sauce to kill both of us."

"Maybe it's your sense of proportion. We know you want to do this slowly and methodically. Diluted to a degree where there'd be no forensic trace. But time is running out. McCloskey is the most hawkish man to occupy the Oval Office since Reagan. He wants his Gorbachev 'tear down that wall' moment with Beijing and he wants it before he leaves office."

"Ah, the all-important legacy," Tommy muttered.

George said, "Look, McCloskey is scheduled to make a major policy statement at the All-Asia Conference in Hong Kong next month. That speech will set the tone for America's position vis-à-vis China for the balance of his term. My people think McCloskey wants an excuse for a showdown with Beijing. So you need to act. Sooner rather than later."

"Okay, fine, sooner. Just give me some time."

"As long as you understand our friends have zero desire to see this president's face at the All-Asia Conference in Hong Kong. It's next month, for God's sake, T. They want their mandate executed. As they put it. The operative word in that sentence being 'executed.' Got it?"

"You think that's news to me? You think I haven't been trying? What is this? You want me discovered? There are mechanisms in place to protect him, navy culinary experts watching the entire kitchen staff. These are people who know the fucking difference between murder and bad shellfish, George. Is that what you want? I don't think so. Fingers pointing at me? I'm a fucking Chinese national, remember? High on the list of likely suspects? You think?"

"I think I've got news for you, my friend. Our Mandarin friends grow impatient. They want this over. Not now, but right now."

"Listen. What the hell am I supposed to do? He's in goddamn Walter Reed Hospital. Surrounded by his Secret Service agents. He's untouchable. Shit."

"Listen to me. You're a goddamn Te-Wu assassin. First in your class at the Xinbu Te-Wu Academy. That's why you got this assignment. Just do what you have to do."

"I will. When and if he gets out of ICU and recovers and comes home, I'll make sure he doesn't just get another really bad case of food poisoning. Trust me. Until next time, okay?"

"No."

"What do you mean, 'No'?"

"Not good enough, my friend. This op is only a small fragment of a far, far bigger picture. The Mandarins are . . . complicated. And the Chinese military's hatred for this goddamn country is reaching a feverish pitch. Someone's got his blood up, and that someone is General Moon."

"Yes, I know. General Moon and his grand plan. Spring Dawn and all that happy horseshit. What is it? When is it? Who the hell knows? I'm just a hired hand in the kitchen."

"Not at all, T. Your reputation and skills are deeply respected. It's just that, here, you have no need to know more. You have your mission, I have mine. Accomplish yours so I can do mine. Now. Understand?"

"Oh, I do, believe me."

"At any rate, we like this guy, Vice President Rosow. The veep seems a far more reasonable fellow than the POTUS. Amenable, let's say. You know, philosophically and politically speaking. We can work with him, is what they think. They want Rosow at that Hong Kong conference. Moreover, and more important, they want Rosow in the Oval, Tommy. ASAP. It took a very long time to get you in position down in that damn kitchen. Now it's time to act. ASAP."

"Don't be an idiot."

"What?"

"No one says ASAP anymore. It's embarrassing."

"Really, Chow? In that case, I'll put it in a phrase even you can understand . . . chop-chop!"

"Does the expression 'go fuck yourself' have any meaning for you, George? That's a question."

"Tommy. Listen to me, you stupid sonofabitch. The world clock is ticking down, little man. Tick-tock. They want this done. Take him out. You've got until noon Friday. That's what they said."

"How the hell am I supposed to get to him when he's propped up in bed over at Walter Reed? Surrounded by Secret Service. I can't fucking do it. And you damn well know it."

It was starting to rain more heavily, a hard cold rain. Unlike his friend, Tommy Chow had no umbrella. The tall, thin State Department man stepped into the street and started trying to hail a taxi, talking to Tommy out of the side of his mouth.

"Not my problem. Thanks for the cocktails, pal. Keep in touch. Oh. Your family back home in sunny Beijing? The PLA guy I work for? He says I'm supposed to tell you they're doing great. Living the good life. Make sure you keep it that way."

"You asshole."

"Yeah. Like you. I fit right in at State that way.

Being an asshole, I learned early, is the perfect credential for an aspiring politician who's for sale. Oh, look. Here's my cab. See you around, T. And don't forget what I said."

He climbed inside the taxi, collapsing his umbrella as he did. As he pulled the door closed, he heard Chow's voice calling.

"Forget what?" the round little man said over the heavy rain.

The thin man stuck his head out the window, smiled, and said, "ASAP."

CHOW TURNED AND walked back to the scant cover of the trees. What he really wanted to do was walk away from the whole thing. Catch a cab to Reagan and board the next thing smoking for Bermuda. He had a bad feeling about this. He had no assurances he'd survive no matter which way this went. He was going to be an inconvenient man when it was over. He should run. Brazil, Argentina. Find a job in a good restaurant and start over. To hell with Beijing and whatever new political catastrophe they were planning . . . he could run.

And then he saw the floating faces of his wife and child. His mother.

And he started walking back to the White House in the pouring rain.

After a while, his step got lighter. He started to

smile as the beginnings of the idea took on shape and substance.

A few moments later, Tommy Chow had a plan.

As soon as he got back to his apartment in Chevy Chase he'd call his handler in England on his encrypted sat phone. She'd help him figure out the details. Once the deed was done, he'd need a lot of cash and a method to get out of the United States and back to his old apartment in London in a hurry. How?

Chyna Moon would make certain arrangements for his speedy exit from the scene of this assassination. After the dust had cleared a bit, he'd make his way home from London, back through Hong Kong and Shanghai to Xinbu Island. Back to his beloved Te-Wu Academy. And start training for the next mission.

Georgie Porgie, that arrogant dickhead, would find out who had the brains around here soon enough. ASAP.

CHAPTER 8

Near Chongjin, North Korea
Present Day

SHE COULD FEEL a thousand eyes upon her, and she
knew not one of them shone with pity.

Kat Chase walked, stumbled, and was dragged relentlessly toward the killing ground. Her torn camp
shift was ragged and bloody from the beating she'd
received upon waking. When they bored of rou-
tine torture, they dragged her kicking and screaming from the cell. She knew where they were taking
her. Had accepted finally that, after years of hell in a
North Korean labor camp, finally, this was the end.

There was to be no heroic last-minute rescue. No
white knights in black helicopters. No. And no U.S.
Cavalry at dawn, fast-roping down from the sky to
save her.

The guards, who stank of fried peppers and onions, screamed at her incessantly, telling her to stop dragging her feet. She was so emotionally numb she barely registered the fists pummeling the crown of her head. She thought her nose may have been broken. It was easier not to even try to breathe through it, so she breathed through her mouth.

There were sharp stones underfoot. Her shoes had disintegrated months ago, and her bloody feet were bound with filthy rags that offered no protection. It was very near dawn, and countless torches flared in the darkness at the bottom of the hill. She could see the heaving black range of mountains rearing up on the far horizon, the sky turning a faint pink beyond them.

Her last sunrise.

At least she could take refuge in the notion that she wasn't going to hell. She was already there.

Through her tears of rage and frustration Kat could see all she needed to see: three guards were pounding a stout wooden stake into the hard stony earth. It was a wheat field, lying high near the edge of a cliff top a few hundred feet above the banks of the Yalu River. The river that marked the border with China.

A large group of ragged, emaciated but excited prisoners had gathered in a semicircle, perhaps a thousand or more, all come to witness the execution. It was a rare treat for the inmates of hell.

The camp commandant's idea of a class play.

The labor camp laws, the "Ten Commandments" laid down by "Babyface" as Kat had come to call the chubby, sadistic, cherubic commandant, forbade any assembly of more than two prisoners. This commandment was waived only for certain festive occasions like this one. Attendance was mandatory. Public killings in the labor camp and the fear they generated were considered teachable moments. Murder for the sake of the public good. She'd been in the audience many times before. Cheering and laughing lest she be shot on the spot.

Now she was the center attraction. The doomed star of the production. And a Caucasian to boot. This was a rare moment not to be missed.

As she drew near the rough-hewn post where she would die, she could hear the despicable little man in charge of the event warming up the crowd.

"This prisoner," he shouted, "this stupid woman about to die, has been offered redemption through hard labor by our dear commandant. But she has proven unworthy of his offer of mercy. She has rejected even the benevolence of our Dear Leader and the great generosity of his North Korean government . . ."

He went on in that vein, but she had stopped listening. She was determined to focus her last thoughts elsewhere. Her husband, William, whom she had loved upon first sight. Her two children, Milo and Sarah, whom she adored beyond measure. In the beginning, in the first few months, they'd allowed her regular contact with them. In the later years, none at all. She had no idea if either of her kids were still alive. Much less her husband.

Since the night long ago, the night of her goddamn fortieth birthday when they'd all been snatched off that foggy street in Georgetown, she really knew nothing of her family. Since they'd been bundled into a black van by Chinese thugs, drugged, and secreted out of the country . . . her family had ceased to exist for her.

She'd see pictures of the two children, every so often, grainy black-and-whites, shot in a camp that very well could have been this one. They did that, she supposed, kept Milo and Sarah alive, only to force compliance with their demands. The pictures were almost worse than nothing. She hardly recognized her children anymore. Thin, hollow-eyed ghosts . . .

A few years ago, she'd managed to steal a picture of Bill from a desktop while she was being interrogated. No idea when it had been taken, but he had more grey hair than the night they'd been abducted. His stomach more paunch than washboard.

He stood out on the deck of an aircraft carrier at sea, demonstrating something or other, surrounded by Chinese naval officers who were laughing at something he'd said. She'd lost fifty pounds. But Bill hadn't changed. If anything, he looked healthier than when he'd been working himself to death back home in Washington.

A thought so horrible it made her sick came unbidden into her mind.

Had her husband defected to China? Had he known about the black limo waiting outside the restaurant the night of her birthday? The van?

She shoved the notion aside for the delusions caused by malnutrition, physical and psychological abuse, and the simple paranoid insanity that it was. And then she blessed her beloved family, each one of them, one at a time, in her heart, and said her final good-byes.

She was tied to the stake, her arms and feet bound behind her. One of the guards pried her jaws apart while another stuffed her mouth full of pebbles from the Yalu River. This was in the revered tradition of preventing the condemned from cursing the state that was about to take her life.

Her head was covered with a filthy burlap sack that still stunk of rotted hay and the human feces they used for manure in the fields . . .

KATHLEEN CHASE HAD spent the last eleven months of her five-year imprisonment in a space reserved for the lowest of the low. An underground prison within the prison. Her stinking windowless room with no table, no chair, no toilet. This was her "punishment" for refusing to admit to her crimes against the state. Admit that she was an American spy. An agent for the CIA come to sow discredit on the government and engineer revolution against the Dear Leader.

The underground prisons were built to blindfold

the prying eyes of American satellites. But not hers. She'd kept her eyes open just in case she ever managed to escape. She memorized the guards who tormented her, their names, their faces, their habits.

She'd learned that for all the prisoners publicly executed in these prisons each year, thousands more were simply tortured to death or secretly murdered by guards in the underground facility where she lived. Rape was a given at any time of day or night. Most prisoners were simply worked to death. Mining coal, farming, sewing military uniforms, or making cement. All the while subsisting on a near-starvation diet of watery corn soup, sour cabbage, and salt.

Issued a set of clothes once a year, prisoners worked and slept in filthy rags. There was no soap in her cell, no socks, no gloves, underclothes, or even toilet paper. Twelve- to fifteen-hour days were mandatory until death.

Over time, if they live long enough, prisoners lose their teeth, their gums turn black, their bones weaken. All this by the age of forty, and none had a life expectancy beyond the age of fifty.

In December, she would turn forty-five . . .

She felt the rough hands all over her body. The guards getting in one last good feel, squeezing her breasts painfully. Then she was alone at the stake. She heard their boots clomping away from her. She heard the low keening noise of the crowd beginning to reach a fevered pitch.

She took a deep breath, knowing it was her last.

Finally at peace, she waited for an eternity or more for the lead slugs to pierce her flesh and find her heart.

She heard the guard captain scream the order to fire.

Fire!

Fire!

Fire!

The crowd saw her head pitch forward, her chin on her chest. A roar went up. Deafening.

But there had been no blood, no twitching corpse riddled with bullets. They'd all fired above her head. She'd heard the rounds whistle above her. She had simply fainted.

This was not the first mock execution the joyous crowd of prisoners had witnessed. They'd seen hundreds. And so they knew the appropriate response. They laughed. Wildly and insanely, letting the guards know they were in on the joke, that they appreciated the entertainment.

"WRITE THE LETTER!" her tormentor screamed at her. She was back in the basement in a private room on the lowest level of hell. Kang was in rare form today, practically frothing at the mouth. He was the only one who spoke enough English to be trusted with interrogation of such a prize as the valuable American woman, Kathleen Chase.

"You write! Tell your husband what happened this morning. About our Dear Leader's beneficence in sparing your life. His mercy. Tell him about your good health. About how well you are being treated here, you and your children. Hot food, good beds. If not—"

"Show me my children, damn you! Show them to me!"

"Your children are alive, we keep telling you. But they will die if you do not obey. They will watch you die before we decapitate them. They will suffer before—tell him. You write the letter now!"

"You write it, Kang. Sign it, too. And then go fuck yourself."

"Bitch!" he screamed. The he raised his fist and slammed it down, the ballpoint pen in his grip piercing her hand, nailing it to the wooden table.

She howled in pain, unable to stop it, but her cries were no longer enough for him. He started slapping her viciously across the face, whipping her head around until she thought she'd pass out again . . .

She no longer believed her two children were alive. She had not seen them in so very long . . .

She had only one hope now.

That next time, the bullets would not miss.

CHAPTER 9

South China Sea

HAWKE DIDN'T HAVE to wait long.

One second all was calm, the next he felt the rippled pressure of sudden underwater movement.

He waited for what always came next.

A soft nudge in the small of his back. No pain, just the tentative probing of some large fish. Exactly just what kind of fish it might be was not a question he preferred to speculate about. But the words just wouldn't go away.

The bad one was *snout*. That's what the nudge had felt like.

Then, a minute later, there was the really bad one. *Shark.*

No mistaking it.

Minutes later, another punishing blow.

Christ. A jarring slam to the rib cage on his right side. A second later, he saw the shark's dorsal fin knifing toward him maybe two seconds before it hit him. Sharp pain now, it hurt like a bastard. Broken ribs in there for sure. He turned slowly in the water, minimizing his movements.

Even in the pitch-black darkness, he could see the dorsal fins circling lazily around him. What did they say about curiosity? Oh, yeah, curiosity killed the pilot. Right now, they weren't in dining mode. Right now they were only curious about this new object in the neighborhood. He took a deep breath, winced at the resulting pain, and let it all out slowly.

This could go either way.

They could get bored with him and just disappear.

Or, the other way, they could shred him into several bite-sized chunks, ripping away his limbs first before fighting over his torso. Staying positive in adverse conditions was one of his main strengths, so that's what he did right now.

The fact that more dorsals were appearing and encircling him, and the fact that his body was suspended, hanging there helplessly in the frigid water, well, that made it tough to stay cheery.

But Alex Hawke, it had to be said, was nothing if not one tough customer.

He closed his eyes and immobilized his body, forcing himself to concentrate on all the good things in his life. His cherished son, named Alexei by his Russian mother, now just four years old. He saw him now, running through the patches of dappled sunlight on the green meadow in Hyde Park. The child's guardian, Nell, was chasing him, laughing. Nell was more than a nanny. She was Hawke's much-loved woman. Something of a legend at Scotland Yard, and in truth, Alexei's bodyguard, Nell had saved the child's life on more than one occasion. Because of Hawke's recent activities in Russia, his son had been targeted by the KGB.

One of his deepest fears was creeping around the edges of his conscious thought. The fear that this night he was leaving his son without a father. Or even a mother. It had happened to him at age seven . . . no other pain can compare.

An hour passed. A very long hour.

For whatever reason, the roll of the dice, God's infinite mercy perhaps, the toothy beasts had left him alone, at least for the moment. Cold had begun to claw its way inside his protective armor. He was shaking now, and his teeth were chattering away, much ado about bloody nothing. It crossed his mind that freezing to death was a far, far better way to go than serving himself up as a midnight snack for the finny denizens of the deep.

He slept, God only knew how long.

And then the lights came on.

Literally.

HE FOUND HIMSELF the target of a shaft of pure white light. He looked up to his left and saw its source.

A searchlight mounted high on the superstructure of a massive ship of some kind. Then another light snapped on, and another and another. Each one picking him out from a different angle.

This must be what it feels like to be some kind of star, he thought, and, cheered that he still had a shred of his sense of humor left, he smiled to himself.

And then he became aware of the deep bass thumping of helicopter rotor blades, above and to the right. He saw the hovering black shadow come closer until it was right above him. An LED spotlight in the chopper's bay winked on and picked him out.

A diver appeared, standing in the bay and looking down at him.

Could this possibly be a friendly? The odds were certainly against it, given China's recent military posturing in this cozy little corner of the world. But, still, if this had to be bad, he'd take China over North Korea in a heartbeat. The NK troops were merciless automatons who brutalized and killed anything that moved.

The diver stepped out into the air and dropped.

He splashed down about ten feet away, surfaced, and started speaking to Hawke in Mandarin Chinese. His hopes for a miracle vanished, but still, it was better than the other option. Hawke spoke enough Mandarin to know he was being told to remain calm and he did. The swimmer approached and began securing the lifting harness to Hawke's semifrozen body.

Hawke had spent a lot of time in China with his

friend and companion Ambrose Congreve, the famous Scotland Yard criminalist. In addition to being a brilliant detective, Ambrose had studied languages at Cambridge. While doing a six-month stint in a Shanghai hoosegow for "subversive activities" that had never been proven, Congreve had given Hawke a basic, working knowledge of Chinese.

"In the nick of time," Hawke said to his savior in his native tongue.

"What?"

"You arrived just in time. I was slowly freezing to death."

"Silence. No conversation, please."

"Have it your way. Just trying to be friendly."

Hawke and the rescuer were winched up and into the belly of the Chinese Changhe Z-8. He lay on his back, shivering. No one aboard would talk to him. He was quite sure they knew about the unidentified aircraft that had entered their airspace and been "shot down" by one of their SAMs. So they were sensibly predisposed not to be chatty. Hell with them—he was still alive, wasn't he? He'd managed to avoid being eaten alive, had he not? Truth was, he'd gotten out of tougher scrapes than this one over the years.

Once the chopper was airborne, he got another surprise. The mammoth floating Good Samaritan, the ship that had stumbled across the downed pilot by the sheerest of luck? It was a bloody carrier! When the chopper set down on the aft deck, he saw, to his utter amazement, an advanced Chinese fighter jet, which was the spitting image of one he'd seen in a meeting at the Pentagon just two years earlier. Code-named "Critter" because of all its spindly appendages, it never went into full production because of government "cost cutting" as the White House chose to describe it.

And now there was a whole flock of the damn things out here in the South China Sea under cover of darkness.

Whatever lay ahead, the spy knew he'd hit the espionage equivalent of the jackpot.

CHAPTER 10

THE INITIAL INTERROGATION aboard the Chinese aircraft carrier was short but brutal. Hawke gave up nothing, and he had gotten out of it with little more than a severely wounded left knee, a few broken ribs, a black eye, three broken fingers, and a concussion. The leg was the worst. Two gorillas had tried to break it by pulling it backward. The attempt failed, but they'd managed to snap a tendon or two. He could walk, but not far.

When they got bored with him, they told him he'd never leave the ship alive, then locked him up inside a stinking crew cabin in the bowels of the bilge with room for little more than a crappy bunk bed.

He now lay on the top berth thinking very seriously about how the hell to escape before these bastards came for him again. Tortured and killed him.

Two military policemen with automatic weapons had delivered him to this charming boudoir. He was fairly certain the same two would come for him when it was time for the more labor-intensive interrogation. They were merely thugs, those two, viciously abusive, but stupid. Just the way he liked them. He'd feigned a far worse concussion than he'd actually suffered, forcing them to half carry him down many flights of steel stairs, something they bitched about all the way down.

At one point they threw him to the deck and took turns kicking at his already damaged rib cage with their steel-toed boots. He'd passed out from the pain.

He was consciously unconscious when they returned. They slammed into the tiny space and manhandled him down from the upper bunk. As he expected, they yanked him to his feet and wrapped his arms around each of their shoulders in order to keep him moving.

He kept his head down, chin bouncing on his chest, mumbling incoherently. When the goon on the left paused to kick open the half-closed door, Hawke took advantage of the moment. His powerful arms reached out with all the speed and precision of two striking cobras as he swept the two men's heads together with sickening force. The collision of the two skulls was sufficiently forceful to cause the two men to drop like sacks of stones to the floor.

He dropped to one knee and checked.

They were dead.

"Hit them too hard," he whispered to himself.

He fished the keys to his handcuffs from one of their pockets and freed his wrists. Then he quickly stripped the uniform from the taller of the two. It fit him badly, but it might be good enough to get him safely up eight flights of metal steps to the carrier's flight deck without hindrance.

Hawke had jet-black hair, which helped, and he kept the military police cap brim pulled down over his eyes, and his face lowered. He also had the advantage of having a fully automatic rifle slung over his shoulder in case things suddenly got spicy.

He raced up as fast as he could without calling undue attention to himself.

A sailor opened a hatch in the bulkhead just as he mounted the last set of steps. He felt a cold blast of icy wind howl in from the flight deck. He waited a full sixty seconds before stepping through the hatch and out onto the flight deck.

He had no earthly idea how he was going to execute the plan he'd devised lying in his bunk, waiting to be tortured again and probably killed. The fact that he didn't know was of little concern. You had to be able to make this stuff up as you went along. He heard laughter and saw a sizable group of men approaching his position.

He retreated and quickly stepped inside the nearest open hatchway. And suddenly found himself inside a large hangar amidships on the flight deck. Unusual, to say the least. Hangars on carriers were always belowdecks. He moved back deeper into the shadows.

A huge shrouded object loomed up in the dim overhead lights.

What the hell?

There was just enough light to see. He'd already formed a pretty good idea of what lay beneath the cover before he began tugging the tarp away.

The thing took his breath away.

It was the Spectre!

Either the supersecret American drone itself, or a perfect facsimile of it. Spectre was a massive, bat-winged, unmanned drone. Half again as large as his F-35C Lightning, and clearly equipped not only for surveillance, but for offensive aerial combat. Slung beneath the sleek, swept-back wings, six very lethal-looking missiles, three to a side.

And, under the fuselage, a bomb the size of which he'd never seen before. A huge bunker-buster? God forbid, a nuke?

A carrier-based drone of this size would be capable of delivering massive devastation from extremely high altitudes from anywhere on the planet. It immediately occurred to him that his entire perception of the world playing field had just altered. If he could e-mail a photo of this thing back home, it would lift Langley off its foundations.

China had somehow managed to leapfrog ahead of the West in terms of military technology and hardware. He knew the U.S. Navy was contemplating a future that included carrier-based drones for combat and delivering nuclear warheads, but China was already there!

How? How in God's name had they managed it?

He heard laughter outside on the deck and rushed back to the open hatchway. He paused, calmed his racing heart, and peered out onto the deck.

Pilots.

There were eight of them, all in flight suits. Some had already donned their red-starred helmets, some were carrying them in their hands. All were kidding around, walking with that unmistakable and cocky jet-jock walk.

Their destination was obvious, Hawke thought. They were crossing the wide expanse of darkened deck, en route to the covey of eight highly advanced fighter jets parked near the starboard bow catapult. Fighters like the one Hawke had seen when the rescue chopper landed on the deck the night before. The pilots would have to pass directly in front of his position.

They represented his only hope of survival.

Hawke remained hidden in the shadows of a massive drone hangar directly beneath the carrier's bridge looming above him. As the pilots approached, their banter continuing, Hawke stood stock-still and held his breath until the last Chinese fighter pilot was safely past his position.

Hawke then stepped out of the shadows and fell

in behind the lone straggler at the rear. Fortunately for him, this pilot was by far the tallest of the lot. He approached his target directly from behind, matching him stride for stride. When he was perhaps a foot behind the pilot, he shot out both hands, and used pressure from both thumbs on the carotid artery to paralyze the poor chap and yet still keep him on his feet.

Giving the main body of hotshots sufficient time to move on, he then quickly withdrew, walking the unconscious man back into the shadows of an AA battery. It was the work of a moment to zip himself inside the pilot's flight suit, don his boots and helmet, and, finally, flip the dark visor down. He then strode quickly, but not too quickly, across the deck, rapidly catching up with the jocular pilots just as they were climbing up into their respective fighters.

He made a beeline straight for the sole unoccupied fighter jet, saluting the two attending deck crewmen who stood aside for him to mount the cockpit ladder.

"Lovely night for flying, boys," he muttered in his guttural Chinese, sliding down into the seat and adjusting his safety harness. After strapping himself in, he reached forward and flipped the switch that lowered the canopy. He then took a long moment to study the instrument array and myriad illuminated controls, quickly deciding exactly what did what.

Looking at the array of aircraft instruments, Hawke was astonished for the second time since arriving up on the carrier's flight deck.

Most of the cockpit controls on the fighter looked oddly familiar. Why? Because they were almost identical to those in the prototype of the top-secret new American fighter jet he had flown, the J-2. He was amused (in one way) to see that the Chinese had stolen so much advanced aeronautical technology from the West that getting the hang of basic things here in the cockpit was embarrassingly easy.

But he had flown the first-generation F-35C Lightning off the USN's *George Washington*'s flight deck courtesy of Captain Garry White and the US Navy. And this Chinese airplane? It was vastly more sophisticated in terms of avionics, communications, and, most important, offensive and defensive weapons systems. Holy God, compared to the current F-35C, this thing was like something from another goddamn planet.

Take the cookies when they're passed, he thought, smiling.

Due to unforeseeable circumstances, a top British intelligence officer was about to take one of what had to be, up until this moment, China's most closely guarded military secrets for a little airborne test drive!

CHAPTER 11

HAWKE GAVE THE internationally required hand signal to the crewmen on deck below and flicked the switch that lit the candle. The sudden engine roar behind him was instant and powerful. He added power and taxied into position behind the last jet in line. The blast shield had already risen from the deck behind the lead jet in the squadron, and Hawke watched calmly as the fighter was catapulted out over the ocean, afterburners glowing white hot.

A wave of pain in his rib cage washed over him and he must have passed out because he suddenly heard the air boss screaming in his headset, telling him to get his ass moving. The aircraft directly in front of him had advanced into position and he'd not followed quickly enough for the air boss. Now he added a touch of power and tucked in where he belonged. There remained only three fighters on the deck ahead of him.

He focused for a second on what to say and how to say it. He not only had to get the Chinese right, the words, but also had to get the attitude right, a slangy mixture of swagger and humble obeisance to the air boss gods on high.

"So sorry, boss," he muttered in the time-honored traditional communicative style of fighter pilots all over the world. For a carrier pilot, the air boss is God himself.

"Don't let it happen again, Passionflower, or I'll kick your sugarcoated ass off this boat and clear back to Shanghai."

"Roger that, sir," Hawke said, advancing a few feet forward.

"You forget something in your preflight, Passion-flower?"

"No, sir," Hawke said, starting to sweat a bit.

"Yeah? Check your goddamn nav lights off-on switch for me, will you? Just humor me."

Shit, he thought, flicking the nav lights switch. He'd actually forgotten to turn his bloody nav lights on! Dumb mistake, and he could not afford to be dumb at this point, not in the slightest.

"You awake down there, boy? I'm inclined to pull your ass right out of the lineup."

"Sir, no, sir! I'm good to go."

"You damn well better be. I've got my eye on you now, honey. You screw up even a little bit on this morning's mission and your ass is mine. You believe me?"

"Sir, I always believe you. Sir. But I'll come back clean, I swear it."

"Damn right you will. Now, you get the hell off my boat, Passionflower. I got more important things to deal with up here than to worry about little pissant pilots like you. Taxi into position. You're up."

Hawke throttled up and engaged the catapult hook inside the track buried in the deck. He heard the blast shield rumbling up into place behind him and looked to his left. He nodded his head, a signal to the launch chief that his aircraft was poised and ready. The chief raised his right arm and dropped it, meaning any second now.

Hawke's right hand immediately went to what fighter jocks fondly call the "oh-shit bar." It was located just inside the canopy and above the instrument display. The reason for the handhold is simple: when a pilot is violently launched into space, the gut reaction is to grab the control stick and try to climb. It's terrifying to feel out of control when the plane's wheels separate from the mother ship. In the tiny amount of time it takes a pilot to move his or her right hand from the oh-shit bar to the joystick, a nanosecond, the catapult has done its job and the pilot can safely assume control of the aircraft.

Adrenaline was pumping, flooding Hawke's veins as he gripped the bar with his right hand. A "cat shot" from a modern carrier is as close as any human being can come to the experience of being in a catastrophic automobile crash and surviving. It was that intense.

The cat fired and he was thrown violently backward, leaving the leading edge of the deck.

He stifled an intense scream of pain at the back of his throat.

He was airborne.

He craned his head around and looked back down at the deck lights of *Varyag*, the carrier growing rapidly smaller as he swiftly gained altitude. He deliberately suppressed any feelings of joy over having escaped an agonizing death at the hands of the most sophisticated torturers on the planet.

He wasn't out of the woods yet, he told himself as he climbed upward to form up with "his" squadron's flight. Their heading was a WNW course that would take them directly over the disputed Paracel Islands. Exactly the wrong direction, in other words. He needed to be on a heading north-northeast and he needed to get moving.

The rim of the earth was edged in violent pink as Hawke slipped into his designated slot at the rear of the tight formation. The squadron leader acknowledged his arrival and went quiet. There was a minimum of radio chat for which he was grateful. There was normally a lot of banter at this stage and he didn't want to hear any questions or inside wisecracks over the radio, things he couldn't respond to without sacrificing his cover.

He needed precious time to remain anonymous

until he could figure out the next step of the plan he'd hatched in those few hours he spent alone and in pain. Namely, how the hell to get away from the squadron without a dogfight. A dogfight that would pit him against seven of China's top guns was a bad bet.

If he simply peeled off and made a run for it, and didn't respond to radio calls, the squadron leader would immediately radio the carrier and report what was going on. One of their pilots was behaving very strangely. It wouldn't take a second for the Chinese carrier skipper to put two and two together: the missing American pilot had somehow gotten inside one of their fighters. He was about to steal it. Blow him out of the sky.

The Chinese would then use the incident as clear-cut proof the West was being deliberately provocative. Instead of preventing a confrontation, Hawke would now be the cause of it. C, to put it mildly, would not be pleased.

They would trot out his blackened corpse and the twisted remnants of the stolen fighter jet on global TV. Use his actions to justify an even more aggressive posture in the region. Take retaliatory measures against Taiwan, Japan, Vietnam.

Next step, war.

That's how he saw it anyway. C might disagree. But C wasn't sitting in the hot seat with his ass on the line.

For the moment, he had little choice.

He flew on, maintaining his slot in the formation,

flying north toward the Pacific Ocean, desperately searching for a means of escape for the second time in twelve hours.

HALF AN HOUR later, battling pain and fatigue, it came to him. It was so simple. The only reason he had not thought of it sooner was the pain of his injuries and mental fatigue. But, he thought, it just might work.

He thumbed the transmit button on his radio.

"Flight Leader, Flight Leader, this is, uh, Passion-flower, over."

"Roger, Passionflower, this is Red Flight Leader. Go ahead, over."

"Experiencing mechanical difficulties, Red Flight Leader. System malfunctions, over."

"State your situation."

"I'm flying hot, sir. Engine overheat. Power loss. Cause unknown. Running override systems checks now. Doesn't look good."

"Are you declaring an emergency?"

"Negative, negative. I think I can throttle back and make it home to mother. Request permission to mission abort and return to the carrier, sir. Over."

"Uh, roger that, Passionflower. Permission to abort. Get back safely. Over."

"Roger that, Red Flight Leader. Returning to the *Varyag*, over."

HAWKE PEELED AWAY from the formation, banked hard right, and went into a steep diving turn away from his flight. The sun was up now, just a sliver above the far horizon, streaks of red light streaking across the sea far below. He looked up and saw Red Flight's multiple contrails streaking across the dawn.

When Red Flight was completely out of visual and radar range, he corrected course to NNE and throttled up. He leveled off at 40,000 feet and took stock of his situation. By his calculations, he could reach his destination in under two hours.

He set a heading for South Korea and stepped on the gas.

His plan was simple.

Contact Kunsan Air Base in South Korea. Home of the American Eighth Fighter Wing, Thirty-Fifth Fighter Squadron, and the Eightieth Fighter Squadron. Tell them exactly who he was, identify his J-2 Chinese fighter, and beg them not to shoot him down. Land. Refuel. Contact C from a secure phone at the base commander's office and tell him his lockbox containing a few million quid were gone to the bottom of the South China Sea. Admiral Tsang would just have to wait.

But he was coming back to England's Lakenheath RAF base with one or two little surprises that might just be worth more than the contents of the lost lockbox.

Infinitely more.

CHAPTER 12

Washington, D.C.

"HAPPY BIRTHDAY, DARLING!" the First Lady trilled.

She swept into his darkened hospital room hidden behind an enormous arrangement of peonies in her favorite shade of pink. She went to the tall windows, threw open the curtains, and cleared a space for the flowers on a dresser top. Watery sunlight flooded the president's room. She considered a moment, then placed the large cut crystal vase overflowing with pink peonies where it would look best.

"What do you think? I arranged them myself."

"Beautiful, honey," the president said, glancing up at her from his slew of binders and briefing papers. "Thanks."

She looked over at him and smiled. A real smile. *Not like the old ones*, he thought, the ones that could barely mask the fear and the pity in her eyes. The ones that confirmed his own darkest nightmares and worst imaginings.

That he was dying.

"How do you feel, birthday boy?"

"Like a million bucks, baby."

"In Confederate bills?" she said, repeating an old joke between them.

"Hell, no. Bona fide U.S. greenbacks, backed by the full faith and credit of the United States government. Namely, me. Not bad for a seventy-year-old coot, sugar."

"Attaboy! You go get 'em, cowboy. There's a new sheriff in town and he's kicking ass and walking tall."

Tom McCloskey laced his fingers behind his head, leaned back against his pillows, and beamed at his lovely wife. She was wearing the sky blue Chanel suit he'd bought her on rue du Faubourg Saint-Honoré in Paris. With the halo of sunlight touching her auburn hair, she looked like an angel. Which, in his humble opinion, she truly was.

He really did feel good, damn it.

In fact, he had made a remarkable recovery since his arrival at Walter Reed Hospital. He was alert, cogent, rational, and in amazingly good humor. His eyes were clear, his skin was radiant. Whatever had been bothering him these last few months, the docs here at Walter Reed were taking care of it. Now he had one overpowering obsession. He was itching to get out of here and get the hell back to work.

The world was blowing up out there. With a lot of help from China and a little added push from North Korea, war was brewing in the Pacific. The Brits had told him they had a three-star admiral in China who'd refused the Kool-Aid. This top naval-ops guy was going to "retard the process." But so far? He hadn't seen dick.

The Middle East, as usual, was on fire. At home, too many people were out of work. The stock market was rocketing toward twenty thousand, and yet the economy still sucked the big one. And he was one of the few people on earth with balls of sufficient size and the power to fix it.

Just last night he'd done a fifteen-minute live bedside interview with Bret Baier, the evening anchor from Fox News. Hard questions, no softballs, that was Bret. China, Japan, Iran, Putin's massive war games. The recent bellicosity of the crazy North Koreans, their threat to nuke Hawaii. And he'd knocked every damn one of Bret's questions out of the park. Short, concise, cogent answers, backed up with an impressive understanding of the details underlying each issue.

Bret was the former White House chief correspondent, incredibly savvy and a hell of a nice guy. All-American kid, just the way he liked them. Clean-cut, he looked like he could have been on the White House Secret Service staff. People had been calling all morning to wish him happy birthday and report that the "Twitter-verse" was abuzz with news of the president's miraculous comeback. The New York Post, they said, was running a front-page photo of him smiling from his bed. They'd Photoshopped a white ten-gallon Stetson on his head. The headline underneath, they said, was "The Comeback Kid!" The copy would talk about how he had his health back, was itching to get back in the saddle, and would be riding tall when he did.

There was a commotion out in the hall, and Mary Taliaferro, one of his favorite nurses, stuck her pretty red head inside the door.

"Mr. President? Just wait till you see what all has shown up out here at the nurses' station. My gosh, you just won't believe it!"

McCloskey laughed and looked at his wife.

"All right, Bonnie, what's this all about? You know I don't like surprises."

"Oh, honey, you know I wouldn't do that. Would I?"

She crossed the room, trying to keep the smile off her face, and pulled it open.

"Oh my goodness, look who's here!"

"Who?" the president said, sitting up and straining to see over her shoulder. "Oh, my Lord, look at that!"

The first thing through the door was a massive four-tier birthday cake. It was on a rolling table, and they wheeled it right up to his bedside. It was decorated to look like his old homestead in Colorado, the Silvermine Ranch. Miniature ranch house on top, stables, paddocks, and two little figures on horseback that looked like Bonnie and him. Even the old blue Scrambler jeep he used to get around the property. Every tier was covered with tall green fir trees, cowboys, and cattle, a tiny version of everything he cherished on this earth.

"Well, boys," he said to the two smiling young Filipino White House waiters, "you guys have outdone yourselves this time. That cake is flat-out beautiful. That big black stallion there even looks just like my own El Alamein."

"Thank you, Mr. President," one of the waiters said. "We are all very proud of it. The entire kitchen and waitstaff has asked me to wish a most joyous and happy birthday . . . and a speedy recovery."

The president starting clapping, and everyone joined in the applause.

His wife bent and kissed his forehead.

"Happy birthday, you big hunk," she whispered in his ear. "You come on home and get your cute little butt back in my bed, okay?"

There was a knock at the door. She smiled, straightened up, and motioned to one of the young Secret Service guys standing just inside the door.

And the next thing he knew, his favorite country singer in the whole world walked through his door. The vice president, the White House chief of staff, and Ken Beer, his personal physician, walked in, followed by about a dozen nurses all crowded inside around his bed. All of them were grinning from ear to ear.

"You've got to be kidding me," the president said.

Damned if it wasn't Bonnie Raitt herself.

Dressed in full cowgirl regalia, Bonnie smiled at him as she walked over to his bedside and she took his hand. She sang, "Happy birthday to you, happy birthday, Mr. President," and proceeded to sing by far the best rendition of "Happy Birthday" he'd ever heard. When she finished, the room erupted into cheers and wild applause once more.

The president's eyes filled with tears.

"Miss Raitt," he said, "I'm going to tell you something. Until this moment, I thought the best version of that song had been sung by Marilyn Monroe to Jack Kennedy at Madison Square Garden. But you know what, you're not only a lot prettier than Marilyn, you're one helluva lot better singer."

Bonnie smiled, put her hands on her hips, and said, "Mr. President? Let's give 'em something to talk about."

And she bent over him and kissed him full on the lips.

Everyone in the room erupted into loud, heartfelt laughter.

"Wow. What a birthday," he said, beaming at his wife. "You are something else, honey. Thank you so much. This means the world to me."

"Let's cut the cake!" she cried.

The younger of the two waiters handed the president a silver cake knife.

The president looked at his cake, beaming. "I don't want to ruin it. Can somebody take a picture first?"

His wife got out her iPhone, starting snapping shots,

and said, "Go on, darling, cut the cake. You get the first bite."

He eyed one of the horses first, but said, "I never cared much for horse meat," popping a frosted chunk into his mouth. "I'll eat the jeep."

And those were the very last words the forty-fifth president of the United States ever said.

The president's head fell forward on his chest.

Ken Beer, his face stricken, pushed his way through the crowd around the bed and bent over the unconscious president.

The president's heart had stopped.

"Nurse!" Ken yelled. "Cardiac arrest! Get the bed down flat. Check his pulse!"

"Ken, what is it?" the First Lady cried, her face a mask of horror. "What's wrong with him?"

The physician plucked a piece of uneaten frosting from the cake, held it under his nose, and sniffed it.

"It's that fucking cake," Ken Beer said, staring at the monitor, which had flatlined. "Damn it! Get the crash cart in here now! There's no cardiac output. Intubate him and start CPR immediately. Who's the head nurse in here? Get all these people out of here."

The Secret Service agent in charge got on his radio, "Rawhide is down! White House to lockdown. Secure the entire kitchen staff immediately. Nobody moves."

An older nurse stepped forward and ordered everyone out of the room except the Secret Service, nurses, doctors, and Ken Beer. "And somebody bag that cake in a HAZMAT container. It's lethal."

Half an hour later, the nurse's compressions on the president's chest ceased.

They all stared at the monitor, and Ken Beer took the president's pulse again.

He ordered shock pads. He ordered one milligram of atropine injected. He did everything he could.

"The patient is asystolic," Ken said, profound sadness inscribed all over his face. "Flatlined. No cardiac output . . ."

The nurses waited. The First Lady had her back to the scene, facing the windows and her peonies. She was visibly shaking. When she heard Ken's voice, she started sobbing silently.

"Okay. Let's call it," he said.

The president's wife looked at his profile, her heart full of regret for all the steps and missteps that had brought them so full of hope and promise to this place and time.

Thomas Winthrop McCloskey, the forty-fifth president of the United States of America, was dead.

Murdered in his own goddamned bed.

"Let's give 'em something to talk about," Bonnie Raitt had said minutes ago.

Within hours, the whole world would be talking.

ABOUT THE AUTHOR

TED BELL is the former Chairman of the board and World-Wide Creative Director of Young & Rubicam, one of the world's largest advertising agencies. He is the *New York Times* bestselling author of *Hawke, Assassin, Pirate, Spy, Tsar, Warlord* and *Phantom*, along with a series of adventure novels for Young Adults. He does most of his writing on an island off the coast of Maine.

www.Facebook.com/TedBellNovels

www.tedbellbooks.com

Visit www.AuthorTracker.com for exclusive information on your favorite HarperCollins authors.